# A TIME
### *for every*
# SEASON

Don Williams

WESTBOW°
PRESS
A DIVISION OF THOMAS NELSON
& ZONDERVAN

Scriptures taken from the Holy Bible, New International Version®,
NIV®. Copyright © 1973, 1978, 1984, 2011 by Biblica, Inc.™ Used by
permission of Zondervan. All rights reserved worldwide. www.zondervan.
com The "NIV" and "New International Version" are trademarks registered
in the United States Patent and Trademark Office by Biblica, Inc.™
All rights reserved

This is a work of fiction. All of the characters, names, incidents,
organizations, and dialogue in this novel are either the products
of the author's imagination or are used fictitiously.

WestBow Press books may be ordered through booksellers or by contacting:

WestBow Press
A Division of Thomas Nelson & Zondervan
1663 Liberty Drive
Bloomington, IN 47403
www.westbowpress.com
1 (866) 928-1240

Because of the dynamic nature of the Internet, any web addresses or
links contained in this book may have changed since publication and
may no longer be valid. The views expressed in this work are solely those
of the author and do not necessarily reflect the views of the publisher,
and the publisher hereby disclaims any responsibility fwor them.

Any people depicted in stock imagery provided by Thinkstock are models,
and such images are being used for illustrative purposes only.
Certain stock imagery © Thinkstock.

ISBN: 978-1-4908-8373-1 (sc)
ISBN: 978-1-4908-8372-4 (e)

Library of Congress Control Number: 2015909304

Print information available on the last page.

WestBow Press rev. date: 7/6/2015

# ACKNOWLEDGEMENTS AND DEDICATION

$\mathcal{U}$ntil writing this book, I never imagined the number of people I would come to rely on to give of their time and talent for something that was not their own. It has been a wonderful confirmation of the kindness of friends. Thanks to Dr. Tia Hughes for her encouragement and expertise in the area of stroke and rehab. To Drs. Zdravko Stefanovic and Ernie Bursey, thanks for their support and technical expertise in biblical studies. Both of these gentlemen also regularly allowed me to speak to their classes about my ideas on Ecclesiastes. The opportunity to explore this book with college students was a gift. For their interest and editorial eye, Yvette Saliba, Stefanie Johnson and Wanda Hopkins. As a gifted writer and editor, and for her knowledge of publishing, thanks to my daughter-in-law, Ashley Williams. Two individuals whose reading and feedback was always an encouragement, my Assistant, Jeanne Townsend and my colleague and, incidentally my uncle, Bob Williams. A special thanks to Lynnet Reiner whose editorial gifts and reader's eye helped the manuscript and my thinking to mature. Even with all of this interest and help, I take full responsibility for the book, its message and its shortcomings.

Finally, to my wonderful wife, Merrie Lyn Williams, I give my undying affection and thanks. Her love, support and advice are the windows through which this work was envisioned and accomplished. It is to her I dedicate this book.

# CHAPTER 1

What do people gain from all their labors at which
they toil under the sun? —Ecclesiastes 1:3

"Daddy."

The voice had a distant, dreamlike quality.

"Daddy?"

It was closer now. He had the fleeting image of a little
girl with long brown hair calling to him.

"Daddy!"

He opened his eyes. His chin was on his chest, and
he saw what looked like his grandfather's hands. Gnarled
knuckles anchored veins that tracked like translucent IV
tubes across the back of each hand.

"Daddy, are you okay?"

He looked up. It was the voice of his daughter, Emma.

"You had me worried," she said in a soft voice anxiety
had squeezed a note higher.

He was tempted to say there was nothing to worry
about, that he had died three months ago and was just
waiting for everyone else to figure it out. But he knew she

wouldn't appreciate his humor. He was where he had been for much of the last month, sitting in his worn leather chair in a corner of the guest bedroom in his daughter's house.

"I'm okay, sweetie. I must have dozed off."

He was dressed in faded tartan-plaid lounge pants with a navy-blue V-neck sweater pulled over a gray tee shirt. On his feet were battered, backless leather slippers. He knew his hair wasn't combed, and a rime of white whiskers dusted his chin. The lounge pants were embarrassingly threadbare. Sarah had tried to get rid of them years ago. They were still here, and she was gone.

"Daddy, can I get you anything?"

He thought for a minute. "How about some grapefruit juice?"

It wasn't that he wanted any. He knew she was trying to be helpful. Anyway, he just wanted to be left alone— at least for a few minutes. Her voice had broken in on memories of happier times. He'd been recalling the last move he and Sarah had made before she went into the nursing home. It had been the perfect home, and their decade there had been sweeter because Sarah's charm had made it a refuge for them and an oasis for the friends and family who stopped by.

Now it was all gone. The house had been sold, Sarah's final illness was over, and he was an old man living out his days in the shelter of someone else's home. What did one do with the threadbare remnants of a life? An acrid emptiness overwhelmed him at times, a gastric reflux of bitterness that was uncharted territory. Not that anyone would notice. He could probably still pull off the calm cheerfulness he had cultivated over a lifetime.

Somewhere around the time he'd turned fifty, he would see old couples walking down the street, and a quiet dread would squeeze his chest—an unwanted, sympathetic nervous system reaction that would quicken his breath and bring a whisper of anxiety. He wondered about their health, their marriage, their love life.

Sarah and he had often joked that they would go out together. They'd told their friends that if the Lord didn't arrange it, they would climb into their car and do a Thelma and Louise. He could picture them hurtling over a cliff. But theirs had been a sensible life, and he knew they would never have done it. The thought, however, gave voice to the dread of one leaving the other behind.

The end had come in the most predictable yet unwelcome way—first the nursing home, then the hospital, and finally hospice. It had been peaceful enough, and he knew that was a blessing. They'd taken advantage of the opportunity to write the final chapter of their lives together and really say good-bye before the lights went out. He was at peace with that.

It was carrying on that he was struggling with. Similar to what they'd felt in their twenties when they'd had more month than money, he now had more years than yearning.

Emma came back with a glass of juice and set it on the table next to his chair. She started to leave, and then sat on the edge of the bed. Her angular frame was still trim, and her once-long brown hair had been cut short. She said it was a concession to her age. He had never understood why older women couldn't wear long hair. Sarah had cut her blonde tresses when she was in her thirties. He'd always missed them.

"Daddy, what can I do to help? You sit here most of every day just staring into space. It's not healthy."

"I know, sweetie. I just don't know what to do. And if I did, I don't know if I would have the energy to do it."

"You've made a lot of progress in the three months since Mom died."

There was a long, pensive silence.

"Why don't you write? You never felt you had the time when you were working. What about that book you started years ago? Why don't you work on that?"

The thought of it filled him with an odd mixture of heaviness and hope. "I'll think about it," he said noncommittally.

Emma looked at him. "Listen," she said. "Now that Chris is home, he could type for you. Your three-finger style takes forever." She smiled.

A slight tilt of the head and a quiet "Hmm" was his only response. With that he closed his eyes again until Emma left the room. When he heard the door click shut, he opened them and thought about what his daughter had said. Maybe he should write. He suspected old age would give him a perspective he'd never had before.

For the first time in over a year, he felt the faint stirring of interest in something other than survival under a blanket of loneliness and grief. The thought of his grandson helping him was a bit daunting. He would enjoy reconnecting with him but knew he needed to be careful given Chris' current state of mind.

He looked across the bedroom at the bookcase he had brought from home and saw the rows of books he'd collected over the years. The mournful lament of the Preacher called out to him. "There is a time for every purpose under heaven … A time to be born and a time to die." He had lived most of the other couplets in that poem—gathering and casting away, loving and hating, rending and sewing, laughing and crying. Was it now his time to die?

*There is a time to speak and a time to be silent*, he thought. The silence would come. Before then maybe he had one more thing to say.

# CHAPTER 2

I have seen all the things that are done
under the sun; all of them are meaningless, a
chasing after wind. —Ecclesiastes 1:14

*I*n the month since he'd come home, Chris felt like
he was in a dance with his mother. She was upset
that the end of her marriage had been the catalyst for
his dropping out of seminary. His reality was more than
he wanted her to bear right now. And so they danced
around the emptiness, around the pain, around the truth.
Approach—avoidance—approach was the cadence they
were moving to. More tangle than tango; more wobble
than waltz.

Lying on the twin bed of his childhood with his old
indie-rock posters on the wall, he was tempted to regress
to fifteen rather than act his age. However, his lanky six-
foot frame barely fit on the mattress, and his twenty-five-
year-old soul refused to let him curl into the fetal position.
It had been hard to move home, but he was grateful for a
place to land while he sorted things out.

"Chris," his mother called softly through the closed door.

"Come in, Mom." He sat up and dangled his feet over the footboard as she opened the door and took a seat in the blue corduroy rocker they'd brought in from the family room.

He met her gaze and waited for her to speak.

Without preamble she said, "Chris, you know your grandpa has been struggling since Grandma died."

He nodded.

"Well, the other day I encouraged him to start writing again on a book he began years ago."

"What's it about?"

"Ecclesiastes."

He wasn't sure he liked where this was headed. "So what's this have to do with me?"

"He's a rotten typist, and I thought maybe you could use your laptop to help him get it written down. Besides, I think he would appreciate the company."

He could tell she was uncomfortable asking for his help. With a sinking feeling, he wondered what else might be on her agenda. "I'm not sure, Mom. I'm just not ready to get into something like this." *Especially something as pessimistic as Ecclesiastes*, he thought.

"Would you at least think about it? Maybe talk with Grandpa and see what he has in mind?"

He thought a moment. "I'll talk with him, but I won't promise anything."

"That's all I ask."

With an encouraging smile, she left the room.

Chris got up and closed the door behind her. He turned and flopped on the bed, chastising himself for not telling his mother why he'd dropped out of seminary. And yet he wasn't sure he fully understood it himself.

He did know that the words "He's gone" from his mother's call six weeks ago had shaken his world. To his surprise, the heat of the anger ignited toward his father had incinerated whatever vestige of faith he had in God.

As his anger abated, he wasn't sure what he felt. Numb wasn't the right word. He wanted to be numb, but what he really felt was an aching void, like one of those lakes where the bottom opens up and all the water drains out in an hour. That was it. His heart felt like a sinkhole. Every emotion but the ache had drained away, and all that was left was a stinking mess of muck from which he'd been unable to extricate himself.

He still wasn't sure why his faith had ended up being collateral damage to an event that had been so anticipated. Maybe Freud was right. Maybe his belief in God had been an infantile search for a father figure who, in his case, had never been there for him. But that explained only part of his loss.

Through the years his faith had served him well. Compared to the glib answers of his postmodern peers, it had given him reasonable answers to the big questions. In his family it had garnered respect. His decision to become a pastor had given his parents bragging rights. In their circle of friends, "My son is going to be a pastor" was almost as impressive as "My son is going into medicine." He had officially become the golden child of the family, and he'd liked the way that felt.

Five months ago he would have never imagined being where he was now. With some embarrassment he recalled his last religious discussion with his best friend, Jim, an atheist. They had been frequent sparring partners in a long-running debate over the existence of God.

Each of their conversations had followed a similar pattern. One would bring up something in the news that either confirmed his position or challenged the other's. Each had seemed unmoved by the other's arguments. Now Chris wondered.

His friend had just been reading about the trial of the man who'd kidnapped and held three young women hostage in Ohio. As Chris remembered it, the conversation had begun with the typical benign lead-in.

"Did you see that the guy who kidnapped those women in Ohio was just sentenced," Jim asked.

Chris knew where this was going but jumped in anyway. "The lowlife got what he deserved."

"I couldn't agree more." His friend paused as if contemplating what to say next. "So tell me, where was your God during those ten years? I mean, how come He didn't send someone to rescue them? And how about the babies? I heard that when one of the girls got pregnant, that Castro guy punched her in the stomach and caused a miscarriage."

"Look," Chris said, "you know what I think about these things. God's heart was breaking more than anyone's. He didn't make the guy do it."

"Why do I find so little comfort in that? If my heart was broken and I could have done something about the situation, I would have. If God's heart was breaking, why didn't He do the same?"

Chris remembered finding it hard to marshal an impassioned defense of God. Incidents like this and worse happened every day. He couldn't explain them all. He had believed in God and knew it was his duty to defend Him, even though he didn't know what to say anymore.

"Listen, I can't explain it. I trust God will someday."

His friend's parting shot hurt. "Someday doesn't do much for those girls."

Looking back on that conversation, he knew he had already been struggling with his faith without even being aware of it. Now that his faith was gone, he wondered whether he could even help his grandfather.

# CHAPTER 3

I hated all the things I had toiled for under
the sun, because I must leave them to the one
who comes after me. —Ecclesiastes 2:18

Two days later the old man heard a knock on his
door and said, "Come in." The blinds were closed
against the morning sun, and the old books he'd brought
with him made the room smell like an attic.

"Mornin', Grandpa." Chris settled comfortably in the
worn leather chair, swinging his right leg over the arm.
He was dressed in cargo shorts, a white tee shirt, and
flip-flops.

"Good morning, Chris." He was sitting at a small
writing desk with a book open in front of him.

"Mom told me you might need my help."

"I do, but I'd like to lay it out so you can think about it."

"Okay."

"You know I've been moping around the house since
I moved in. And I know what I'm going through takes

time. But your mother had a great idea the other day, and I thought you could help me follow through on it."

"What do you have in mind?"

"I want your help in writing a book. But I need more than a scribe. I need a muse, someone I can bounce ideas off, someone who will challenge me and cross swords with me when I'm headed in the wrong direction."

He sensed a hesitation on his grandson's part.

"I know it's asking a lot, but I really can't do it without some help. The thing I'm worried about is whether you feel up to jumping into the lion's den with me."

"To be honest," Chris said, "I'm torn. There's nothing I'd like better than helping you. But I'm on really shaky ground right now when it comes to the Bible. I'm going to need some time to think about it." With that he gave a little shrug and a sheepish grin and said, "I'm sorry."

"I respect that. Take all the time you need. Could you shut the door?" he asked Chris as he got up to leave.

In the dim light of his room, he moved from his desk to the old leather chair. He hadn't wanted to show it, but he was very disappointed. Working again on the book had captured his imagination and lifted his spirits. With Chris's reluctance he felt as if he had tripped while backing away from the project. He could feel himself in a free fall, dreading what would happen when he hit bottom. Writing the book, he realized with growing disappointment, was a faded dream – a good idea whose time had come and gone a long time ago.

\* \* \* \* \*

Walking back through the kitchen, Chris opened the refrigerator looking for something to eat. Finding nothing there, he went to the pantry and grabbed a piece of his mother's coffee cake. Pouring himself a glass of milk, he went to the living room, where he turned on the TV and began channel surfing. He found reruns of *Magnum, P. I.* and *The A-Team*, something on the Cooking Channel, a soap opera, and the talking heads on CNN. *What a wasteland*, he thought.

Unwillingly his mind kept flitting back to the earlier conversation. He knew he was right to be cautious but hated disappointing his grandfather. A half hour later, with the milk and cake gone, he hadn't found anything that captured his interest for more than a few minutes.

Picking up the empty glass and plate, he carried them out to the kitchen, rinsed them, and put them in the dishwasher. Walking into his bedroom, he grabbed his car keys off the dresser and headed out. He wasn't sure where he was going, but he had to get out of the house.

\* \* \* \* \*

Late one morning several days later, Chris came into the kitchen and was surprised to see his grandpa sitting in front of a half cup of coffee. Other than at the occasional meal, Chris rarely saw his grandpa outside his bedroom. Chris noticed that his bathrobe hung open over his pinstriped pajamas and that its belt hung by one loop and was dragging on the floor.

"How's it going Grandpa?"

The old man looked up, apparently not having seen him come into the room.

"What?"

"How's it going?"

There was a long pause, and Chris wondered if his grandpa was beginning to lose it.

Finally he said, "Fine. You?"

"Okay," Chris replied. Several seconds of uncomfortable silence passed. "What are you up to today?"

The old man stood up with his coffee cup in his hand. Looking at Chris, he said with a trace of irony in his voice, "First I'm going to make a pilgrimage out to the mailbox. And when I get back, I'm climbing into the leather time machine in my room to take a nap."

After he caught the wry drift in his grandfather's words, the only thing Chris could think of to say was, "Have fun."

Picking up his keys he walked out to his car.

# CHAPTER 4

*There is a time for everything ... a time to embrace and
a time to refrain from embracing.*
—Ecclesiastes 3:1a, 5

That evening, when she had finished brushing her teeth, Emma looked at herself in the mirror. Her hair had the soft, comfortable look of having been brushed and not styled. She liked the feel of her freshly scrubbed face after taking off her makeup.

What she hated were her eyes. She could live with the puffy little bags and crinkled skin that had appeared a couple of year ago. But they had become careful sentinels guarding her inmost feelings, even from herself at times. Gone were the playfulness and purpose that had been such a natural part of who she was. Like stepping onto a cold floor with bare feet, their emptiness sent a shiver up her spine.

Putting her toothbrush into its holder, she turned toward the door. As she did, she slid her index finger along the smooth surface of the second sink. How different it was from how it had been for so many years. No dried spots of shaving cream. No smudges of toothpaste negligently left behind. It was too clean—unnaturally clean.

Turning out the light, she walked through the bedroom and into the hall by the dim light from her walk-in closet. The house was quiet. Chris and her dad had both gone to bed. As she entered the kitchen, she turned on the small lamp at the kitchen table.

Pulling out her ladder-back chair, she sat down, tucking her right leg under her. *Some people have comfort food*, she thought. *This is my comfort place.*

The circle of light acted like a blue screen in a TV studio. Images were projected in the theater of her mind. Seeing the new-moon-shaped dents at what had been her daughter Kristen's place at the table, she remembered her pounding its oak top with her spoon at the age of three. She could see Chris in his Cub Scout uniform, wolfing down his supper before heading off to his den meeting. And there was her husband Gil standing at the counter with his back to them, mixing a smoothie with his industrial-sized blender during his last diet.

Her eyes burned with the tearless fatigue of insomnia. Since being alone, it had been hard to make herself lie down in an empty bed. And if she awoke in the middle of the night, she might as well get up. Her mind accelerated to full speed within minutes. She worried about what was going to happen to the house in the divorce. How were Kristen and Bill really doing out in Seattle? And now there were Chris and her father to be concerned for. On the worst nights she replayed the final act of her marriage, reliving all the anger, fear, and humiliation she'd felt when

Gil slammed the front door as he walked out for the final time.

She got up and fixed herself a cup of herbal tea. As she did so, she looked around the kitchen and smiled at the finger paintings anchored to the refrigerator door sent to her by her two grandchildren. On the back of the chair across from her was the windbreaker Chris had put there when he came home from work. She wished she could as easily take off the layers of his defenses and see what was going on in his heart. It had been a shock when he dropped out of grad school after Gil left. Even though it wasn't her infidelity that had ended the marriage, she felt to blame for its impact on her son.

What was she responsible for? She hadn't let herself go. Two pregnancies had thickened her waist, but she had worked hard at staying fit, even if she wasn't as trim as she used to be. She remembered her horror at finding the first gray hair when she was in her thirties. She'd first eliminated those little enemies of time with weekly search-and-destroy missions. Finally she and her hairdresser had done rinses to cover them up. One day, after Gil's second marital lapse, she'd given up and let her hair go salt and pepper.

Standing by the sink, she realized she had a stranglehold on her cup of tea as she thought about all that had gone wrong. How could a relationship that had seemed so right end so badly? By the time they were into their second decade, she'd known the marriage was at risk. Gil's career was taking off, and she and the kids were a distraction to him. His work as a chemical salesman took him on the road several nights a week. As a broker for industrial raw materials, he worked from home and found it difficult to keep clear boundaries between work and family.

She had gone back to work as an elementary school teacher when Chris started school. When Chris was in Little League and Kristen was in ballet, the responsibility fell largely on her to be the "soccer mom". It was easier to manage the domestic side of life when her work and holiday schedules were the same as the kids'.

Looking back on it now, that had been the beginning of the end. Gil didn't have to make a commitment to the family. He could invest himself in his career because she was there all the time. She never called him on it until it was too late.

In the second decade of marriage, they fell into bed at night like two workhorses after having taken off their harnesses. Gone were the baby doll pajamas and the times when he would wrap his arms around her and whisper naughty things in her ear. By their fifteenth year, she slept in ratty tee shirts and pajama bottoms, he in boxers. After a goodnight kiss, they rolled away from each other and quickly fell asleep.

She wondered whether the mattress industry knew what they had done to romance when they invented the king-size bed. The double bed of their early marriage hadn't let them stray very far from each other. They laughed that their broken-down mattress with the valley in the middle would keep them close, even when they fought. At that age they'd been content to fall asleep spooning. Eventually, even the mattress told their story. When she put on the clean sheets each week, she could see the three-foot gap between the indentations their bodies made night after night.

She suppressed a yawn that made her eyes water. *Enough psychoanalysis for one night*, she thought. Making sense of her life would have to wait. It was time to try to sleep.

# CHAPTER 5

I know that there is nothing better for people than to be
happy and to do good while they live.
—Ecclesiastes 3:12

*E*ven though Emma had invited her father numerous
times, he never went to church with her. He said it
was too difficult for an old preacher to listen to someone
else's sermons.

As she came out of her bedroom, dressed for church
that morning, she sat down next to her father while he
finished breakfast. "Any progress with Chris on your
book?"

"He seems to have my procrastination gene because
he's still thinking about it. I don't want to push it. He's
obviously not ready for this yet."

Her son's attitude really irritated Emma. "Let me talk
with him."

"I wish you wouldn't. I don't need someone dragged
into helping me."

"We'll see," was all she would say as she got up from the table, picked up her purse and headed off to church.

When she returned home a couple of hours later, Chris was just grabbing a bite to eat before heading out.

With a touch of exasperation in her voice, she said, "Chris, why can't you give your grandfather an answer on his book?"

He stopped midbite and looked at his mom. When he finished chewing, he said, "I just don't think I can do it. When I left the seminary, I vowed to put all that behind me. Helping him would bring it all back."

"At this point, I don't think it's about you. You've seen how he is. Many days he doesn't even change out of his pajamas. I haven't had a decent conversation with him in over a week. I think this book could really make a difference."

Reluctantly he agreed to talk with his grandpa again.

\* \* \* \* \*

After wrestling with the situation for a couple of days, he showed up one morning at his grandfather's door. "May I come in?" he asked.

"Sure, have a seat."

He went to the desk, pulled the chair around to the side, and sat on it backwards. Wrapping his arms around the back, he said, "I've been thinking a lot about your offer and have decided to accept."

"Has your mother been talking with you?"

"She has, but this is a decision I made on my own. I realized my problem was with God, not you. Besides,

Ecclesiastes is such a different kind of book. I decided to give it a try."

"I will agree under one condition."

"What's that?"

"That you promise always to be honest with me. If you have a problem with what we are doing, you will tell me."

"Agreed."

* * * * *

Later that week they took what would become their regular seats: the old man in the leather chair and Chris at the desk with his laptop.

"Tell me what you know about Ecclesiastes," the old man began.

"Well," he said with a trace of a smile, "next to Song of Solomon, which is about sex, it is the most dangerous book in the Bible."

"Why do you think it's so dangerous?"

"That's easy. It was written by someone pretending to be King Solomon. It contradicts itself all the time, and it's so pessimistic that it almost wasn't included in the Bible."

"Those are certainly views held by some scholars. I probably wouldn't have put it quite that way, but I couldn't disagree with your characterization."

"So you agree with me," the young man said with a note of surprise in his voice.

"Not exactly. I don't think it's dangerous because of its apparent contradictions but because it's so honest. It's the book of the Bible that gives me the clearest picture of reality."

Turning the small desk and chair around to face his grandfather, Chris began typing notes on his computer.

For the first time since his wife died, the old man wasn't consumed with his grief. Sitting there in his old leather chair, wearing his old leather slippers, he felt as timeless as the book they were contemplating—he, the optimistic realist, facing the disappointed idealist.

"I'll tell you why I want to do this book. I want to write about something that takes an unblinking look at life. At the same time I want something that doesn't just challenge readers but in the end encourages them. Ecclesiastes can do that. It isn't a pie-in-the-sky kind of book."

"But Grandpa, isn't all religion pie in the sky? It's a wonderful ideal, but it has no connection with reality."

"That's my point. Ecclesiastes has nothing to do with religion. That's why it's a dangerous book. That's why I can't leave it alone. Where else in the Bible do you find such truth, such philosophy, such faith?"

"Faith? The author had no faith. He wasn't sure if there was a heaven. He thought humans were no better than animals. Where is the faith in that?"

The sparring stopped as the friendly combatants sat quietly in their corners, considering their next move.

"But Chris, don't you see? To hold onto faith in the face of those mysteries is a beautiful thing. That's what the author has done."

The old man loved nothing better than a good debate with someone with a sharp mind and strong opinions. How he had missed that.

The young man felt a twinge of regret that he had been so honest with his grandfather. He had intended to play his cards close to the vest, and now he had already thrown several down on the table. In spite of that, it felt really good. He looked up at his grandpa to see whether he had shocked him. What he saw was a smile on his face and a sparkle in his eye that he hadn't seen in a long time.

"So how are we going to do this?" Chris asked.

"Well, as you know, I started this book a long time ago. I have been going over my notes and think we can go through Ecclesiastes systematically with you taking what I have written and typing and polishing it a bit."

Chris paused. "I don't know. Do you think that would work?"

"Let's get into it and see. For next time, let's look at an idea I had on how to approach the book."

That drew a nod from his grandson, and the two parted.

# CHAPTER 6

Two are better than one, because they have a
good return for their labor. —Ecclesiastes 4:9

It was 6:30 in the morning. The old man was sitting at the kitchen table in his pajamas and bathrobe. Emma finished buttering the toast and put it on the table with the scrambled eggs. When she sat down, he asked whether she would like him to bless the food. She agreed. They bowed their heads while he did.

The old man could sense his daughter watching him carefully to check on his disposition. He knew she was hopeful that the writing project would cheer him up.

"How did your first session with Chris go?" Emma asked as she put a forkful of eggs on her toast.

"It was good. We generated a few sparks, some smoke, and a little light. I had a great time."

The conversation lapsed as they ate. He sat with his elbows on the table to steady his hand, that had a tendency to shake a little. While he wasn't a hypochondriac, he'd always had a finely tuned feel for his body and wondered whether he was getting Parkinson's. The problem was, at seventy-eight he couldn't figure out what normal was anymore.

Looking at his daughter over his cup of coffee, he confessed to her that for the first time in a long time he felt better. The comment brought a sweet Mona Lisa-like smile to her face. She blinked away the tears that couldn't decide whether to fall.

"I thought I detected a spring in your step," she said.

He laughed. "You would think I'd just returned from a year at sea. These legs of mine can't seem to plot a straight line. That wasn't a spring in my step—it was a stagger in my stride." They both smiled. His little wordplay seemed to confirm the reality of his improved mood.

After another comfortable silence, he shared with her his hope that Ecclesiastes might be just the thing to open her son up. "You know how men are. They always need to have something to do in order to have a good talk. I learned more about life by working on cars with your grandfather than at any other time. Besides, it's too honest of a book, and the issues are too relevant not to produce some good conversations."

"I'm glad for the two of you. I just hope he'll open up to me sometime."

"That will come. I don't think we can rush it."

Emma got up and cleared the table. By 7:15 she was out the door and off to school.

The old man sat at the table a little longer and then shuffled off to his bedroom to get ready for the day.

When Chris came into his room at ten o'clock, he had already found an old file with an introduction to Ecclesiastes he'd written years ago.

Once his grandson was seated at the desk, he began. "Your grandma and I visited the Coventry Cathedral in 1973. The story of its bombing during the war and its rebuilding in the sixties captivated both of us. At the front of the new sanctuary was a tennis-court-sized tapestry that had been woven on a loom in France. We discovered that the weavers never saw the front of the tapestry. They worked completely from the back. Years later it occurred to me that I had in that story a great model for understanding Ecclesiastes.

"Chris, think about the tapestries you've seen. Compared to the clarity and beauty of the front, someone who had only seen the back would have an incomplete idea of the patterns and colors that are so obvious on the other side. I think that's like Ecclesiastes."

Handing Chris two sheets of legal-size paper written in pencil, he said, "Take a look at this and see if you can do something with it."

Chris read the notes, thought about them for a while, and began typing on his laptop. When he was done, he read what he had written and passed the laptop to his grandfather.

Ecclesiastes: Counsel for Living in a Broken World

## Introduction

Many commentaries on Ecclesiastes begin with the observation that it is one of the most difficult books in the Bible to understand. In addition to its seeming lack of organization and contradictory ideas, the author of Ecclesiastes presents a challenging vision of life under the sun.

A way to understand the book is to think of it like a tapestry. In particular, two aspects of tapestries are helpful: how they are viewed and how they are made. These works of art are typically viewed as they hang on a wall. In that way the clarity of the design and the power of the colors are revealed. If one was to go to a store to buy one and it was hung backside out, a request would be made to turn it around.

Humanity's understanding of life under the sun as portrayed in the book of Ecclesiastes is like viewing a tapestry from the back. There is no clear pattern of what is going on. Maddening little hints and subtle indications of the larger purpose of life are there, but that is the most that can be said. And there is no way to ask for the tapestry to be turned around.

On the other hand, the Preacher, as the author of the book is called, believes only God has the front-side view of life and its meaning. Humans might long to see the big picture, but only God knows it.

The second aspect of tapestries that aids in an understanding of Ecclesiastes is how they are made. Threads of particular colors and qualities are strung the length of the loom. Woven back and forth from the sides are other threads arranged to complete its design.

So it is with the themes of Ecclesiastes. Running one way are the threads of injustice, disappointment, and futility. Running the other way are the threads of hope and joy and meaning. Woven together they comprise the warp and woof of life under the sun.

The limited view of life humans have is reflected in the unique structure of the book. Dark threads of discouragement appear and seemingly disappear at random only to appear again later. The same is true of the threads of hope and light. They seem to disappear for long periods of time. And when one thinks there is no hope, they appear again.

The old man stopped reading and said, "I think the readers of our book will have to read Ecclesiastes. If they just go by what we're telling them, they'll be lost."

"They probably will."

The old man began reading again.

The Preacher was writing to more than just believers. He was writing to the person who had seen too much of life, to the pilgrim who had evolved from the innocence of childhood through the optimism of young adulthood, to the pessimism of old age.

He begins the book by stating in chapter one, "I have seen all that is done under the sun, and behold it is all vanity" (1:3). The English word *vanity* comes from the Hebrew word *hevel*, which comes from the root for "vapor" or "fog." Since the Preacher will be taking such a dark view of life, perhaps the word *smog* would work better. It is the combination of something ephemeral, such as a morning mist, mixed with the smoke of despair. Ecclesiastes is a biblical dense-smog advisory.

While this seems like an unusual attitude for a book of the Bible, it provides the nonbeliever and the thinking believer with a meditation on the injustices of life. It addresses the nagging problem of how a good, all-powerful God can be respected in spite of the evil of the world. Other books of the Bible share their answers. It is left to the Preacher to admit that there are no easy ones.

If simple answers weren't readily available to the Preacher, at least he could present realistic ones. He did it not by reconciling the contradictory aspects of life but by holding on to them whether they could be harmonized or not.

"What do you think?" Chris asked.

"I like it. It needs a little work, but it's a good start."

"You know that philosophers would call the Preacher's approach a dialectic where opposing views are presented and may only be understood in tension with each other."

"For a long time," his grandfather replied, "it was a puzzle to me that the author made little or no attempt at harmonization. It wasn't until I got onto the tapestry metaphor that I realized there was no reconciliation to be made. The goal seemed to be to weave the picture and let it be."

The young man stood up. "I need to start getting ready for work," he said.

"Thanks for your help, Chris."

Nodding in response, he picked up his laptop and headed to his room.

# CHAPTER 7

The sleep of a laborer is sweet, whether they
eat little or much. —Ecclesiastes 5:12

After a light lunch, the old man went back to his
room to take a nap. The double bed was a four-poster painted white. It had been Sarah's when she was
a little girl. When they got married, it was the one piece
of furniture she had brought from home. When Emma
was born, it became her bed, and as with her mom, it had
followed her when she moved out on her own.

A patchwork quilt, made by Sarah when their
granddaughter was born, covered the bed. He could still
identify the green-and-white-striped cotton from curtains
she had made for the kids' room. Another section was
from a smock Sarah had sewn for Emma when she started
school.

As he stretched out on the quilt, he wondered why
Ecclesiastes had always fascinated him. He suspected
it was a counterbalance to the optimism he'd always
had. However, since his Pollyanna approach to life had

been challenged so often, he suspected he was more into avoidance than blessed with optimism.

He wondered whether the corollary to the joke that pessimists were never disappointed was that optimists frequently were. Maybe that was why he'd avoided facing the negative. He always counseled, "Hope for the best." It was as if he had to spin the dirty water out of every situation to make it tolerable. He chuckled wryly to himself. Maybe he had come up with a new definition for spin doctor.

And what had his optimism gained him? He was a great encourager, but he also allowed tough situations to fester until they couldn't be ignored. His children called him a terminal optimist. The name was said in love, but even they understood his unwillingness to see the bad, think the bad, or face the bad in life.

His conflict avoidance had been a never-ending source of frustration in his marriage. The last big fight he had with Sarah began with some inconsequential incident that had escalated into her oft-repeated charge that he needed to do something about whatever the situation was.

Always the assertive one, Sarah had said, "If you don't confront this, I will, and you won't be happy with what I do about it."

His answered that he was thinking about it.

To which she responded, "You've been thinking about it for three weeks now." And it took off from there, with no more resolution than any of their previous fights.

With a sigh he concluded that Ecclesiastes wasn't just theology for him; it was therapy. It gave voice to the difficult things in life. When it spoke of crooked things not being made straight or the preference of funerals over parties, it was an antibiotic to the optimism he was infected with, an alternative to the "happily ever after" ending he tacked onto every story.

His mind slowly wound down, and his breathing deepened. His fingers twitched as he drifted across the hidden boundary between wakefulness and sleep.

The domestic sounds of Emma preparing supper brought him gently back over that line: the wheezy whistle of the refrigerator door opening, the terra-cotta sound of dishes being taken out of the cupboard, something being chopped on the cutting board. The smell of onions in the frying pan finally propelled him out of bed and into the kitchen. He was grateful that his sense of smell was one of the last to fade.

"How was work?" he asked as he sat at the table.

"The kids were great. The parents were something else."

"What happened?"

"Oh, I don't know," she said as she stir-fried some veggies. "I've been working hard preparing the kids for their state exams coming up next week, and then I get sidewalked by a bulldozer mother after class today. She wondered why her daughter had to do so much homework. 'Wasn't I the teacher?' she demanded. I reminded her that fourth-graders do bring work home sometimes. Well, that wasn't a satisfactory answer. Didn't I know that her little angel was in ballet and piano?"

"So what did you say?"

"Apparently nothing meaningful. She huffed off with a parting shot: 'We'll see about this.'"

"I'm sorry." He avoided his natural tendency to become the mother's spin doctor, explaining or excusing her lack of appreciation. He knew no matter how tempting it was, there was nothing he could say to make it better.

"I just think I'm running on fumes right now. Hopefully it will get better after next week."

She spooned the stir-fry into a bowl. "Daddy, could you set the table?"

"Sure."

After the blessing, they ate together in comfortable silence.

"Have you heard anything from Gil's lawyer?" The old man's question broke the silence and pierced Emma's heart.

Putting down her fork, she closed her eyes as tears ran down beside her nose, following the worry lines beside her mouth. She wiped them off her chin before they dropped onto her plate.

"I forgot to mention that I was served papers at lunch."

She pushed back her chair and went into the bathroom. He had lost his appetite as well. Picking up their plates, he carried them over to the sink and rinsed them off. He upbraided himself, muttering under his breath, "Nothing worse than an old man without filters."

He sat down at the table, pitching a tent with his arms and putting his head in his hands. Emma came back into the kitchen, blowing her nose. Putting the tissue in her pocket, she walked over and put her hand gently on her father's shoulder.

"Don't beat yourself up, Daddy," she said quietly." There was no way you could have known. It means a lot to me that you're here and that we have each other."

# CHAPTER 8

What advantage have the wise over
fools? —Ecclesiastes 6:8

The bedroom door was open and he heard a light tap on the jamb.

"Come in, Chris."

His grandson entered, laid his laptop on the desk, and sprawled heavily in the desk chair. Waiting a minute to see whether the young man wanted to say something, he asked, "Shall we get started?"

When there was no answer, he pulled out his notes and said, "Why don't we start with the theme of Ecclesiastes?" He paused. "I'm not surprised most people believe it's about vanity. Why wouldn't they? The word is repeated five times in the second verse of the first chapter.

"I believe this five-fold repetition ramps his observation about life to the extreme. Like they said in the seventies, it's futile to the max. Or it's utterly senseless or meaningless or vaporous, depending on how you translate the word *hevel*. But I believe he's giving us the context for understanding life, not the theme of the book.

"It's in the next verse that the Preacher identifies the purpose of the book. He says he is trying to answer the question 'What are we doing here?' Or, better yet, 'What are we supposed to do while we're here?' He'll spend the rest of the book working out the answer."

Looking up expectantly at his grandson, he waited to see whether there was a response to what he'd said. Chris's eyes were locked on the keyboard as he typed with a firmness that belied his quietness.

"What's going on, Chris?"

"Nothing," he said.

Watching him a little longer, his grandfather went on. "The Preacher spends the next eight verses with a little poem that identifies the threads he will weave together as part of his answer. The challenge I'm going to have is to make this section interesting. The thoughts are relevant, but I think most people will get turned off by the idea of a poem."

He paused again, looking at the wiry frame hunched over the computer.

"The poem has two stanzas: one about nature, the other about human nature. Both will make the same points: life under the sun can seem pointless and unsatisfying with no long-term reward."

At that the young man stopped typing, straightened, and looked at his grandfather.

"Okay. Enough about a pointless life in a pointless book," Chris said with some heat. Taking a minute to collect himself, he said, "I know Mom told you she was served papers yesterday."

His grandpa nodded.

Chris continued. "It's like I've got some weird form of PTSD. When I heard that news, all the anger I had when he first left came flooding back. I know how to deal with my feelings toward my father. That's only part of what's going on. It's how I feel toward God that has me stumped."

He took a deep breath and let it out slowly. "I'm really angry with a God I'm not sure I believe in, and I don't know what to do with that." He shook his head and laughed humorlessly.

"It's like seeing the remnants of light from a star that died a long time ago." He thought a minute. "Or maybe it's just safer than being angry with my dad."

"So where does all this leave you now?"

"Confused and mad at myself."

"Why?"

"For believing that stuff in the first place. Then for allowing someone I no longer believe in to rile me up like this."

"Don't we all have our opinions of whether God exists? It seems to me we need to be humble about how closely we think our belief reflects reality."

"But isn't religion about certainty and trust?" Chris said.

"For me it's about humility and trust."

"I don't know what you mean."

The old man thought a minute and said, "I think we need to be humble because there is so much we don't understand. The trust comes in when we put what we believe on the line. In living my beliefs, I come to trust whether they are true."

The quiet that followed was devoid of strain.

"Look, Chris, I like to speculate as much as the next person. But a very wise man once told me to spend the majority of my time living what I believe, not exploring what I don't."

The young man had no response.

"We can stop here if you want."

"No. Let's go on. The distraction is helpful. Sorry about losing it."

"That's okay. I'm upset myself and worried about your mother."

"Me too."

The old man picked up his notes and said, "I guess the Preacher was right. Sometimes life feels pretty futile."

Ignoring that, Chris said, "So how does this poem fit with vanity and the question the writer is trying to answer?"

"The Preacher is saying that to understand life, we must accept the fact that there is little that satisfies and much that is futile. Even if we make a contribution, it won't be remembered long."

"No wonder some of the guys putting the Bible together thought Ecclesiastes ought to be left out. That's about as bleak and depressing a view of life as I've heard in a long time."

"But Chris, don't forget that the tapestry has threads running both ways. We will see some golden threads of hope and faith as well. We just have to look for them."

Chris refrained from further comment as the old optimist and the young idealist called it a day.

# CHAPTER 9

For who knows what is good for a person in life,
during the few and meaningless days they pass
through like a shadow. —Ecclesiastes 6:12

That night the old man dreamed that he and Sarah were in their home. In it he was both a character and his conscious self wondering how Sarah had come back to life. First, hope quickened his heart, but then it dissolved into despair. He awoke, saying her name with tears tickling his ears.

For a several weeks after she died, he imagined he saw her downtown or at the mall. He would hear a voice and think it was hers. Now she visited only in dreams filled with love and longing. As disturbing as the dreams were, he dreaded the time when even they would be gone and he would have to work at remembering the sound of her voice.

Something in the dream triggered the memory of a time when Sarah was still in the nursing home. By then she rarely knew who he was. As with the other women in her family, her body had outlasted her mind.

During a visit to the nursing home one afternoon, an LPN who frequently cared for Sarah called him over to the nurses' station. She asked him whether he knew his wife believed one of the male Alzheimer's patients was her husband. When he said no, she told him that the night shift aide had discovered Sarah asleep in bed with the gentleman several times that week. Each time they woke her and brought her back to her own room, only to have the incident happen again.

The old man realized the nurses at the station were watching for his reaction. Not wanting to upset them, he smiled, and they relaxed a little. What he had heard so far, however, was only the prologue of the story.

The nurse continued, "Just this morning I went in to get Sarah up and found her dressed in that gentleman's boxer shorts and tee shirt. He could see the twinkle of suppressed laughter in her eyes.

She went on, "Without saying a word to her, I left Sarah and hurried down to the gentleman's room. There in bed was this eighty-four-year-old man sound asleep in Sarah's pink nightgown."

He chuckled at the visual that formed in his mind. The nurse gave a relieved laugh as well and told him she thought Sarah believed she had spent the night with him.

"I'm sure that's true," he said before continuing down the hall to his wife's room.

She was dressed in a light-green velour jumpsuit with white tennis shoes. Her hair, now a cottony silver, was brushed back in small waves that framed her face.

Approaching her chair, he pulled up another so he could face her while he held her hand.

Looking at him with a question in her eyes, she tilted her head and asked, "Do you know my husband?"

As he lay in bed that night, he smiled with the joy of knowing that somewhere deep inside she had known him. And he cried with the sweet sadness for all they had shared and all he had lost.

# CHAPTER 10

Consider what God has done: who can straighten what he has made crooked. —Ecclesiastes 7:13

*W*hen the old man came out of his room on Sunday morning, Emma was already fixing breakfast. She looked up from the stove and nodded toward a small stack of papers on the counter.

"Chris left you those with a note."

Two fingers from his left hand slid along the table like an outrigger as he walked by. Turning right, he walked carefully to the counter. Picking up the papers with one hand, he placed the other palm down on the counter. Looking at the penciled note on top, he read, "Grandpa, I did some work on the poem in Ecclesiastes chapter one. Look it over and see what you think. Also, when we talk next, I want to give you my ideas on vanity. Chris."

He put the note down and turned around, leaning back on the counter.

Emma said, "Dad, I'm worried. Chris didn't come home Friday night. He slept a good part of Saturday and was out again late last night." She spoke quietly. "He's in his room asleep now. I'm not sure when he had a chance to write anything."

Slowly walking the five feet to the kitchen table, the old man lowered himself into the chair with an audible grunt. "I'm sorry to hear that. I wonder if he isn't struggling with the divorce."

"I think there's a lot we don't know," Emma remarked as she dished up a plate of scrambled eggs and toast for her father. They ate thoughtful in silence.

\* \* \* \* \*

Sitting in his leather chair later that morning, he laid Chris's draft on the lapboard he often used when working away from his desk. He had made it himself and was quite attached to it. He was never more content than when he was sitting in his leather chair with a good book resting on his lapboard. In fact, it was in that place where he had first begun his work on Ecclesiastes years before. It had been in a different home and a different time in his life, but he felt a great peace as he looked down and began to read.

> If one were to weave the tapestry of life, what threads should be used? Should it be woven with the mauve colors of love and the reds of passion? Would the whites represent courage or purity? Gold and silver might indicate wealth or power.

> How would one represent pain or discouragement or loss? Should they be woven in with the reds and whites and golds? Would the picture portrayed be simple or complex, representational or symbolic?

As the Preacher weaves his story of life, he begins by anchoring the dark threads of life in a broken world. He calls it life "under the sun," and the reader will find that the Preacher will take a hard, honest look at that life. The tapestry will be so troubling and unsatisfying in some places that one will wonder whether there is any light or love or joy woven in.

It begins as a poem—a simple one with two stanzas. It is woven in a herringbone pattern. Dark threads descend inch by inch before returning back to where they began.

> Generations come and generations go, but the earth remains forever.
> The sun rises and the sun sets and hurries back to where it rises.
> The wind blows to the south and turns to the north; round and round it goes, ever returning on its course.
> All streams flow into the sea, yet the sea is never full. To the place the streams come from, there they return again. (Eccl. 1:4–7)

The first stanza looks at patterns in nature. It begins by observing the comings and goings of generations with little trace of their passing. It then identifies meaningless cycles in nature. The earth spins like a top, and with each turn the sun rises and sets only to rise again the next time around. Wind creates its own meaningless dervishes from dust devils to trade winds to hurricanes. The final threads in this stanza represent the insatiable nature of the sea, which never fills and is never satisfied.

Woven next to the threads from nature are those in the stanza about humanity. The experiences of mankind are woven in patterns running parallel to those of impersonal nature.

All things are wearisome, more than one can say. The eye never has enough of seeing, nor the ear its fill of hearing.

What has been will be again, what has been done will be done again; there is nothing new under the sun.

Is there anything of which one can say, "Look! This is something new"? It was here already, long ago; it was here before our time.

No one remembers the former generations, and even those yet to come will not be remembered by those who follow them. (Eccl. 1:8–11)

The threads of the sea run parallel to those of the eye and the ear—none of which are ever satisfied. The Preacher then dashes the hubris of the person who thinks what he or she has done is new or startling. With a yawn, he states someone's new idea is as original as the sun coming up for the billionth time. Finally he completes the poem with a closing bracket about remembrance. As with all things in nature, no matter how significant the life, it will pass and fade from memory.

And so the Preacher begins to weave his story. It is neither happy nor satisfying because it is lived in the mist, in the fog, in the smog of a broken world.

The old man carefully laid the papers down on the lapboard. He closed his eyes and tipped his head onto the back of his chair. It wasn't a bad start to the book. He sighed as he thought about his grandson. What were the themes and threads being woven into his life? He wished he knew.

Now that he was working his way out of his deep grief, he found he could focus on the needs of others for the first time in quite a while. He was really hopeful that he could build a bridge to wherever his grandson was and help him find his way back.

Seeing Chris's willingness to engage with him on the book, the old man began to think about how to pull him further into the project. He needed to have Chris understand he was a partner, not just a scribe. He had told him that in the beginning, but he needed to show it now by using his knowledge of the book to ask the right questions, not to give what he thought might be the right answers. In doing so, he hoped their time together would be a dialogue, not a recording session.

If his approach was successful, the old man would bring Emma into the sessions—not just to get her perspective but to draw her into the relationships that were being built. He hoped it would all work.

# CHAPTER 11

Do not be overrighteous, neither be overwise—why destroy yourself? Do not be overwicked, and do not be a fool—why die before your time. —Ecclesiastes 7:16–17

When Chris woke up on Sunday, he wasn't sure what time it was. He had drawn the shades in his room, and in the unnatural dusk he glanced at the bedside clock and saw it was noon. Gently turning his head back, he looked at the ceiling. Any quick movement made him feel as if someone had drained some spinal fluid and his brain was bouncing off the inside of his skull.

He'd lived the last couple of days in a fog. On Friday night he'd gone to a bar with some coworkers. He hadn't done much drinking in high school, and once he'd decided to be a pastor, he hadn't drunk at all. Now that he was free of all that, he was ready to explore some new approaches to life.

Like himself, his coworkers at the bookstore were young, intellectual, and hip. Any given day would find them in dark skinny jeans, black lace-up shoes, and rumpled button-down shirts with tails that hung out. Several sported scruffy beards, and their shaggy hair was just long enough that it had to be periodically swept out of their eyes and could easily be tucked behind their ears.

Chris's easy charm had quickly integrated him into this new circle of friends, and in the relaxed atmosphere of the bar, he'd been able to enjoy himself for the first time in months. The smell of spilled beer and the loud music would take some getting used to, but there was an intimacy in the tall-backed booths and accepting atmosphere that appealed to him.

When the bar closed at 2:00 a.m., they moved to the apartment of one of the young ladies. None of them was drunk, just loose, and the conversation quickly picked up where it had left off. It ranged from current events to recent movies and, of course, books read.

Each kept pulling a smart phone out of a pocket and texting back and forth to friends—each one, that is, except Chris, whose recent life changes had morphed the landscape of his relationships. He had no one to text.

As he lay in bed that Sunday morning, he thought back to the great time he'd had on Friday night. By the time he got back to his mother's home on Saturday, it was early morning, and he went straight to bed. Later that afternoon, he woke up and grabbed a bite to eat. Finding a new circle of friends was the first inkling that he might actually have a normal, happy life post seminary. Maybe his life-changing decision would actually work out.

The good feeling from the night before inspired him to work on his grandfather's manuscript. He was just finishing up when he heard a car horn outside. He quickly printed the document, left it with a note on the kitchen counter, and headed out to spend the evening with his new friends.

They met at a different bar and spent a good part of the evening talking philosophy. At one point he told them he was helping his grandfather with some writing on Ecclesiastes. Some had a vague knowledge of it from their religious upbringing, but none knew much.

"Post modernism, really," Chris said. "It is about a guy who tries to find his own truth and to experiment with what life is all about. Some of it is kind of depressing really. He wrestles with the fact that life isn't fair and in the end concludes that all is just mist that quickly burns away."

One of the others said, "Cool. I had no idea that was in the Bible. I thought it was just a bunch of myths and 'Thus saith the Lords.'"

"Oh, there is a lot of that too. This book is different. To be honest, I'm only doing it to help out my grandpa. My grandma died three months ago, and he needs something to help him through his grief."

They all nodded in sympathy.

"Anyway, I have to say it has been fun so far."

The conversation turned to what had brought Chris back to town. He hesitated to say too much, so he told them only that he'd been in graduate school until his mom needed him to come home after his dad moved out.

Each then shared the trajectory of events that had led to working at the bookstore. As the evening progressed, the pitchers of beer kept coming, and pretty soon all but the designated driver were pretty far gone. The last hour before they headed home consisted of hilarious storytelling and laughter about things that didn't seem quite as funny the next day.

Now, as he sat up in bed and put his feet on the floor, his head began to throb. As he thought about the night before, it was still a mystery to him why feeling trashed the next morning was worth bragging about. Feeling wasted wasn't that appealing. Time would tell whether he could get into the bar scene. Gently pushing himself to his feet, he carefully shrugged into his clothes and headed off for work.

# CHAPTER 12

So I turned my mind to understand, to
investigate and to search out wisdom and the
scheme of things. —Ecclesiastes 7:25

The next couple of days were quiet. Emma worked in her garden on Sunday afternoon. Roses were a particular love of hers. When she came in at three o'clock to cool down and get a glass of iced tea, the house was silent. It had been that way quite a bit lately. This afternoon the house exuded a peaceful somnolence. Emma imagined her home breathing a long, deep sigh after the months of cold silence and hot argument.

The emptiness and ennui she'd felt right after Gil left were slowly resolving into some form of normalcy. From fixing food to cleaning house, the little routines of life were helping her adjust to her new reality.

The one regret she had was that she hadn't kicked him out. What type of woman, she wondered, let her cheating husband back into her bed? It was hard for her to admit, but she was that woman. Looking back, she was ashamed that she'd allowed herself to be treated that poorly. Keeping the family together was an explanation that went only so far.

At the deepest level she'd come to believe she had no options. Who would want an aging, jilted woman? Even more troubling was the question she was unwilling to answer even now. What was it about living alone that was so frightening?

She'd never imagined being alone; she'd never wanted to be alone and had never chosen to be alone. And yet she was. Or was she? She thought about the men in her life now. Each was going through his own transition.

Just last week she and Chris had sat at this table, talking about a young mother who'd come into the bookstore with her two preschoolers. They'd been looking for *Goodnight Moon*. He found it for them as well as several other books Emma had read to him and his sister when they were that age. With gentleness in his voice, he thanked her for the hours they'd spent sitting on the couch in their pajamas, reading books. Those were, he said, the golden memories of his childhood.

*Oh, to capture those moments*, Emma thought. To be able to travel back in time and relive them with the savor of perspective she had now. They'd been special when they happened. But young parents had no real objectivity, she concluded. They were too close to it all, too responsible. All she could do now was remember. It seemed ironic that the scenery of life was always more beautiful in the rearview mirror.

But what lay ahead for her? She knew that to move ahead she had to come to terms with her issues. Boy, how she hated that term. Along with *dysfunctional* and *enabling*, it represented the worst of pop psychology. She asked herself what she really meant by *issues*. She realized she would have to face herself to be able to face her future. She thought, *who am I apart from wife and mother? Is there enough of me left to build on?* That was the real question, she decided.

Finishing her tea, she put on her gardening gloves and headed back outside.

\* \* \* \* \*

The old man spent the afternoon working in his room. The bright light of the late spring afternoon was hard on his eyes. His optometrist told him bright light would be a problem until he had his cataracts removed. In spite of that, he had the drapes open so he could watch Emma working in the dappled sunlight of the yard. He realized he experienced as much contentment watching her as he had working in the garden himself.

Looking at the open Bible before him and the blank legal pad next to it, he was wrestling with something he'd thought about for a long time—what to do with the experiment the Preacher had recorded in Ecclesiastes 2. What had always stumped him was its modern feel. He'd always had a hard time reconciling this experiment with principles in the rest of the Bible.

Maybe it all struck too close to home. In the old man's mind, people could be divided into two groups—those who learned from others' experiences and those who had to find things out for themselves. The Preacher was clearly in the second group. His own children represented both groups. Emma would watch and read and question and learn. Her brother never took anyone's word for anything. Nothing was true unless it was discovered firsthand. In the end this was his undoing.

He reread the first verses of the Preacher's experiment. "I said to myself, 'Come now, I will test you with pleasure to find out what is good.' But that also proved to be meaningless. 'Laughter,' I said, 'is madness. And what does pleasure accomplish?' I tried cheering myself with wine, and embracing folly—my mind still guiding me with wisdom. I wanted to see what was good for people to do under the heavens during the few days of their lives."

The old man concluded he was more like his daughter—a watcher and a ponderer, one who thought before he spoke and worried too much about what others thought. On the other hand, he'd known a number of people who'd unwittingly lived the Preacher's experiment. He'd never known it to work.

And yet here was a respected biblical character calmly explaining his exploration of madness and folly, his pursuit of pleasure and possessions with an abandon the Preacher himself called "vanity." And how could he claim this was all done under the control of a mind guided by wisdom?

If Solomon was the Preacher, as was traditionally believed, the experiment certainly reflected his life. He'd been given the gift of wisdom, he'd become wealthy, and he'd built Israel into a world-class power. But where did it get him? Did the seven hundred wives and three hundred concubines bring him happiness? Did he find meaning in all his labors? Could he claim at the end of the day that his experiment had been successful?

The old man thought about his grandson and wondered what he would think of all this. He laid down his Bible and began writing some notes for his conversation with Chris. This would be very interesting, he suspected. His concern was to be able to preserve the intellectual engagement without losing the spiritual exploration on a personal level.

\* \* \* \* \*

Little was seen of Chris that week. Each day after work he joined his friends at the bar, returning home only after the others had gone to bed. He never realized that his mother lay awake every night until she heard him come home. Each morning he slept late, showered, grabbed something to eat, poked his head in to say hi to his grandpa, and took off for work again.

In the quiet moments of his day, however, he wondered what was drawing him to his grandpa's book. Given his resolution to put all things religious behind him, the amount of time he was spending on the project surprised him.

He did feel satisfaction helping his grandpa out of his grief, but the more he thought about it, the more he realized there was something else pulling him into Ecclesiastes. It was creating a context for the questions he was asking: a way to face the meaninglessness and despair he feared were his lot now that he'd abandoned his faith. When the sense of being part of something larger than himself was gone, when the simple answers no longer satisfied, where would he find meaning? Even though he and the Preacher were heading in different directions, they seemed to be on the same path.

# CHAPTER 13

This I have found: God created mankind
upright, but they have gone in search of
many schemes. —Ecclesiastes 7:29

"So what do you think?"

The old man and his grandson had taken their places in the bedroom. They hadn't worked together on the book for over a week. The young man had just presented his view that vanity in the book of Ecclesiastes usually meant meaninglessness.

"I don't know, Chris. I kind of like the idea of some form of vapor. That is its root meaning."

"My issue isn't that it might mean 'vapor' sometimes. I just think you're limiting the range of meaning the Preacher had for *hevel*. Look, just in chapter two I can see both of our points. Verse eleven could mean 'mist' when he says, 'I considered my work … and all was vanity and striving after wind.'"

"That clearly seems to mean I worked hard, and it all passed away," the old man said.

"True, but verse fifteen says that the fact that the wise man and the fool both come to the same end is *hevel*. And verse twenty-one says that it is *hevel* when the wise man works with wisdom and then has to leave what he has accomplished for someone who has not labored for it. I don't think either of these can mean mist or even smog."

The old man thought a minute and said reluctantly, "You may be right."

"Grandpa, I know I'm right. There is some dark stuff here."

"Maybe fog and smog appeal to me because of where I am in life. We've all heard old people say how quickly life passes. I can identify with the Preacher now more than ever. Look here."

He picked up his Bible, turned to Ecclesiastes, and began to read. "'For who knows what is good for a person in life, during the few and meaningless days they pass through like a shadow? Who can tell them what will happen under the sun after they are gone?'

"That is chapter six, verse twelve, and it seems to me that even though *hevel* is translated as 'meaningless,' it is so because life is so ephemeral."

"Is that your New International Version?" Chris asked.

"Yes, other versions translate *hevel* as 'futile.' Either way the fleeting nature of life comes through. I can relate to that."

"So maybe we're both seeing the book from our own perspective," Chris responded. "At twenty-five, life doesn't seem to be flitting by me. It does seem pretty meaningless at times."

They paused, both deep in thought.

"Look," said Chris, "the larger question seems to be, can this one book mean something different to two readers? Does it become so broad that it is *hevel*? Maybe it's like a Rorschach test, which is so subjective that it has no meaning outside the personal."

The old man thought a moment. "Or perhaps it's like one of those portraits that no matter where you stand in the room, it appears to be looking right at you. We would say that's the result of the artist's skill. I think the same is true for Ecclesiastes. It is the skill of the artist—in this case God—that it means something wherever you are in life."

Without hesitation Chris responded, "I'm going to have to be convinced of that."

His grandpa smiled. "Listen, up to this point we have fallen into the trap of cherry-picking verses throughout the book. It is one of the most common mistakes people make. I think we need to look at it in order. It was in understanding the structure and organization of the book that it really began to make sense to me."

"That may be good for you, but how are you going to get your readers to take the plunge?"

"I haven't figured that out yet."

"Grandpa, before we leave *hevel*, I want to say one more thing, and I don't want to hurt your feelings"

"Okay."

"What you are proposing about mist and vapor flies in the face of what all of us in this family have just experienced—the loss of the love of your life, Mom and Dad splitting up, and my life taking an about-face.

Doesn't the Preacher say somewhere that the righteous and the wicked many times get what the other deserves?"

"Chapter eight, verse fourteen."

Chris looked carefully at his grandfather. "Have you memorized the whole book?"

"I would call it a working knowledge."

"This is my point. You didn't deserve to be left alone. Mom certainly didn't deserve what she got. I could have used a better father. Life isn't fair. So much of what happens shows there is no larger purpose, no grand plan, and no planner. I think there is room for that view even in Ecclesiastes."

The old man paused. "I think you're mixing up your personal views with those in the book. It is one thing to say it might speak to each of us in the context of our lives. It is another thing altogether to read into it what we want it to say.

"And we can't forget the counterpoint in the book. The Preacher doesn't think everything is pointless. Over and over he says that work and love and even food and wine are not only good but gifts from God."

Even though he had his laptop, Chris hadn't been taking notes. For several minutes both sat there for a while, looking past each other.

"Well," the old man said, "perhaps that is enough for today."

\* \* \* \* \*

When he got back to his room, Chris texted his old debating friend, *"Call me."*

He and Jim had talked once right after he'd moved home. Currently a PhD student in psychology, Jim remained one of the few people Chris could be completely honest with. A little while later, his phone rang. It was Jim.

"Hey, dude. How's it going?" Chris asked.

"Not bad. I'm just starting to study for my written comps coming up in July. It's a little scary. They expect us to know everything. What's new with you?"

"I told you my grandpa was living with Mom and me. Well, I've started to help him write a book."

"Really? What's it on?"

Chris chuckled. "You won't believe this—it's on Ecclesiastes."

"Wow. How's that going?"

"Actually, not too bad. I was thinking today that his and my discussions reminded me of the ones you and I used to have. This time I get to play the loyal opposition."

It was Jim's turn to laugh. "I'm still trying to wrap my mind around the fact that my old buddy Chris has come over to the dark side. So tell me, what's it like playing Jimmy boy's role? I hope I have been a good mentor."

"It's kinda nice not having to defend God every time something bad happens. But I have to say there is something about Ecclesiastes that resonates with me."

"I understand. Back in the day when I was really into religion, it was my favorite book of the Bible. I still think about some of its great lines like, 'Don't be overrighteous neither be overwise, why destroy yourself.'"

Chris surprised himself by saying, "Chapter seven, verse sixteen."

"You are into it," replied his friend. "Maybe you took that verse to heart and got out of seminary before it was too late."

"Hadn't thought of that, but you could be right."

"So, Chris, tell me where you are in your journey from faith to reason."

"I guess you know as well as anyone the struggles I was having, probably even before I did. What you don't know is that it was my parents' divorce that did me in."

"How so?"

"I think I wasn't just angry with my dad. I was angry that God had allowed it to happen. In the end I had to accept the fact that either God didn't care enough to do something or that there was no God to the rescue."

"That's rough," Jim said.

"Maybe that's why the book of Ecclesiastes is so appealing to me right now. The author isn't afraid to say we don't have a clue about so many things. I guess I was enamored by the belief that my faith had the answer to all the big questions. When I found out it didn't, it all began to crumble. The divorce was just the final blow."

There was a long enough pause on the other end that Chris asked, "Are you still there?"

"Yeah, man. I'm just thinking. I understand not liking the fact that God may be responsible for some bad things. That isn't the same as not believing in Him. Take it from me; you've only taken the first step."

"What do you mean?"

"When I first started to question the existence of God, I was really rejecting the answers my faith was giving me. I wasn't yet at the point of rejecting the source of those answers. Believe me, you have a long way to go. I'm at a point now that if I was in a foxhole, I would still be an atheist."

His friend's insight troubled Chris. He'd convinced himself that he was at the end of the road and didn't want to hear the trip had just begun.

"Hey, man," Chris said, "I've got to run. I'll keep you posted on what's going on. Good luck with your exams."

With that they hung up.

# CHAPTER 14

While I was searching but not finding—I found one upright man among a thousand, but not one upright woman among them all. —Ecclesiastes 7:28

That night when Emma came home from school, her dad was sitting at the kitchen table. After she dropped her briefcase in the office and changed into jeans and a cotton blouse, she came back to the kitchen. She hadn't seen him just sitting for a couple of weeks, but here he was: at the table with no books or writing pad in front of him. She came around the table and stood behind him with her hands resting lightly on his shoulders.

"Is everything all right?" she quietly asked.

"I'm fine," he responded. He reached up and squeezed one of her hands. "I've been working on my book most of the day and was waiting for you to come home so I could tell you how much I appreciate your suggestion that I start writing again."

Emma could feel his thin shoulders through the light-blue denim shirt. His once-athletic build was slowly wasting away. She noticed his hair was thinning on the crown of his head. Reaching up, she smoothed a wispy strand that was so fine she could barely feel it.

"I'm glad," she said. "I can see the difference. For one thing your appetite is better, and you actually spend time outside your room now."

She went to her chair and pulled it back across the braided rug lying under the kitchen table. Before she sat down, she walked over to the stove, took the teakettle, filled it with water, put it on the back burner, and turned it on high.

"Can I get you anything, Dad?"

"I'm good."

"Tell me how the book is going."

"That's actually what I wanted to talk with you about," he said. "I need your perspective on a couple of things and wondered if you would be willing to spend some time with me on it."

"You know I'd love to. I've been dying to know what has been going on in there when you and Chris are working."

"I would like you, me, and Chris to sit down together, but I'm not sure he's ready for that yet. I'll talk with him and see what he thinks. In the meantime—" He stopped midsentence as the teakettle started to whistle.

Emma got up and took her favorite cup from where it hung under the cupboard. She turned off the burner and, reaching into a small ceramic tray on the counter, got a packet of orange pekoe. Placing the bag in the cup, she filled it with hot water, brought it back to the table, and sat down.

As she dunked the tea bag up and down in her cup, her father continued, "In the meantime, I'd like to pick your brain."

"I'm all yours."

"I want to start with you where I started with Chris. Tell me what you know about Ecclesiastes."

She thought a minute. "Well, I know a rock group used some of the verses for a hit song in the sixties."

"That was the Byrds with *Turn! Turn! Turn!* Most people don't know Pete Seeger wrote the song. What else?"

Emma stood up, got a saucer and spoon, and returned to her seat while she thought. "I remember some of your sermons on it when I was a kid. I always wondered why *vanity* was used so much. At first I thought the Bible was talking about a nightstand. Later, when I knew that *vanity* meant 'conceited,' that still didn't help.

"As a teenager I remember trying to read it and getting more confused. Now I only remember two verses. One was from a sermon you once preached. I remember you quoting something from Ecclesiastes about time and chance happening to all people. I was intrigued but didn't know what to make of it." She pulled the tea bag out of her cup, squeezed it out on the spoon, and set both of them on the saucer.

"What was the other verse?"

"'Remember your creator in the days of your youth.' Now that one made sense to me." She smiled.

"If you want to help, you're going to have to read it again. Can you do that?"

"Sure."

"Thanks. So here is what I'm wondering. Would you ever pick up a book about Ecclesiastes and read it?"

"I doubt it," she said with a slight shrug.

"Okay, let me ask it this way. What would make you want to pick up a book about Ecclesiastes or any other book of the Bible, for that matter?"

"Well, I'm not sure," she said with some hesitancy.

"Emma, you aren't going to hurt my feelings. Nor is your opinion going to keep me from working on my book."

Finally she said, "At this point in my life I want my spirituality to be practical. I don't want things scholarly, but I want to know the author isn't riding his hobbyhorse. So I guess I want things fresh and with enough meat to get me thinking. In the end I would keep reading a book that is a blessing and an encouragement."

"Thanks, sweetie. I appreciate your honesty."

Later that night as he was getting ready for bed, he thought about the challenge of his daughter's words. He knew the Preacher's message had him so captivated that he needed the input of someone like Emma or Chris so he wouldn't write a book only he would read.

* * * * *

After getting ready for bed, Emma sat cross-legged on the bed in her pajamas. She had her feet tucked under the edge of the blanket and her Bible open on her lap. She knew Ecclesiastes wasn't long and decided to read it in one sitting.

A half hour later she closed the Bible and leaned back against the pillow she had propped against the headboard.

Closing her eyes, she thought about what she'd just read. She could see why the book so captivated her father. It was occasionally practical, sometimes maddeningly complex, and many times obscure. It was the perfect book to spend a lifetime contemplating.

The first thing she'd have to deal with was the cynical attitude toward women. Was this guy a woman hater or what? She couldn't believe he'd said in chapter seven that he found one good man in a thousand but not one good woman. Given the trajectory of her marriage, she would have reversed those figures.

Perhaps Gil had been on a similar journey as the author—a desperate thrashing about in an attempt to fill a void. As she thought about it, however, she refused to grant him that. Any explanation for bad behavior seemed to justify it. Maybe the experiment in chapter two was just a philosophical rationalization for men acting badly. She realized she would need to be careful not to project too much of her own stuff onto the story.

Putting that aside, she wondered what to do with what seemed like a schizophrenic view of life. Was the author a workaholic, or did he love his work? Was wisdom a good thing or something to drive you mad? And where was God in all this? The author's approach was so different from any other book in the Bible. She decided it would be good to dig a little deeper with her dad and see what the book might say to her.

Laying her Bible on the nightstand, she turned off the light, slipped under the covers, and did her best to go to sleep.

# CHAPTER 15

Who is like the wise? Who knows the
explanation of things? —Ecclesiastes 8:1

At supper two nights later, Emma and her father agreed to spend some time talking about Ecclesiastes. After the table was cleared, she went to get her Bible. When she came into his room, her father was already sitting in his chair with his lapboard and Bible. She sat at the desk where Chris usually sat.

"Where do you want to start?" he asked.

"I'm tempted to pick your brain about the author's attitude toward women. But I'm going to have to sort out some personal things before I can address that. You know my practical bent. If I don't see how it applies to my life, I have a hard time paying any attention to something. So what I need to know first off is how the picture of God in Ecclesiastes fits in with the rest of the Bible? I can't decide whether this guy believes in the same God I do."

"He does, but he doesn't."

"What do you mean?"

"It's pretty clear he has a more limited view of God than we do today. I'm not sure he would have stood out that much in his day, however. For one thing, there wasn't a clearly developed view of the Devil back then. Everything that happened was seen as an act of God.

"Even in the book of Job, where Satan has a much clearer role than any other book in the Old Testament, Job is heard to say to his wife in chapter two, 'You are talking like a foolish woman. Shall we accept good from God, and not trouble?'"

"Okay, I can see that. But it's more than that in Ecclesiastes. For one thing God seems to come and go. He's barely mentioned in the first two chapters. Then He shows up big-time in chapter three. Then He disappears in chapter four, only to show up in chapter five. He then disappears in chapter six and reappears in chapter seven. I don't get it."

"Emma, I have proposed a way of looking at Ecclesiastes that I think would help you here. I think we need to see this like a tapestry with ideas woven into the book. In this case the picture of God comes and goes like a thread or pattern in a tapestry."

"But why do it that way? If what you said earlier is true, that people back then saw God in charge of everything, wouldn't He be in every chapter?"

"You would think so. But the author of Ecclesiastes—Chris and I call him 'the Preacher'—has a different approach to his writing. He wants to contrast life with God and life without God. In my mind this is how he has organized the book. I like to think of it as a loose weave, not a tight weave. A lot of commentators have tried to use key words or the number of verses in a section to create an outline. I think that is a mistake. It's too prescriptive, and that wasn't the goal of the Preacher.

"He is more interested in moving us back and forth between the counterpoints of life, what Chris calls 'a dialectic.' He begins by introducing the major threads or themes in chapter one. Chapter two tells of his experiment to discover what worked in life. The end of chapter two and all of chapter three present the first counterpoint. Up until then he presented the brokenness of life, where work and possessions and pleasure are seen as vanity. Putting God squarely in the picture, starting in chapter two, verse twenty-four, changes everything.

"In chapter four he begins his first series of proverbs, just sensible but somewhat pessimistic advice for living in a broken world. It is good advice, whether one believes in God or not. Then in chapter five he brings God back in but in some very practical ways about making vows and going to the temple. As you have pointed out, this back and forth is pretty clear throughout the rest of the book."

"So let me see if I got this right. The Preacher, as you call him, may have a broader audience than the typical book of the Bible. He isn't writing just for the religious readers of his day. And because of that, he tells some of what God is doing, but in other chapters he just wants to give guidance to his readers, even if they don't care that much about God. Is that right?"

"That's the way I see it. This problem of the contrast between the sections has led a lot of scholars to believe there is more than one author. A common view is that the real author is the pessimistic one who says little or nothing about God. It is proposed that the God talk may have been added by a pious editor to make the book presentable to a religious audience."

Emma thought about this and said, "But you are proposing that there is one author with a diverse audience in mind. I can see that. But for the practical reader like me, how does that apply to my life today? It's nice to know the readers of the Preacher's day could relate, but what can it say to me today?"

"That's the sixty-four-thousand-dollar question. I think of it in two ways. One, the Preacher hopes to reach any reader of any time with an honest picture of life. For you at this point in your life, he is saying, 'Emma, sometimes life stinks. It's not fair, and people don't always get what they deserve.' Hopefully that honesty would draw you into the book."

"Okay. But where does it go from there?"

"That's my second point. Once he lays out his case that life isn't always fair, he then weaves in a picture of God as the One who knows what is going on and who has given us some pretty simple blessings, such as work and family, to get us through those tough times. The Preacher is saying that if we can see those as gifts of God and know He is with us in those gifts, we will be better able to ride out the tough times.

"I think a good example is his portrayal of work in chapter two. Just count the number of times the Preacher says 'I' or uses some other personal pronoun. It is all about him, and in the end he believes it's all vanity. He worked hard, but for what purpose? Accumulation? To have more than the next guy? That selfish perspective on work burned him out. Then at the end of chapter two, he brings God into the picture and says the only way work can be a beautiful thing in your life is to see it as a gift of God. That can make all the difference."

"I remember seeing that," Emma replied. "The frustrating thing for me is that he tells us these things are gifts but doesn't elaborate on what that actually means. They're gifts – so what?"

"Do you remember Tolstoy's opening line in *Anna Karenina*? 'Happy families are all alike. Every unhappy family is unhappy in its own way.' I think that idea applies here as well. Life can go wrong in so many ways but can go right in only a few simple ways. Putting God in the picture of work or family is no formula. It is an attitude, an openness to His blessing and guidance. The Preacher isn't able to elaborate the ways in which that would be so for each person. He can only state that for life, work, or family to be beautiful, we must recognize God's role in them."

"So it's like what you always say about Murphy's Law," Emma said. "It's true because there are so many ways that something can go wrong but only one way that it can go right."

"Exactly. After the Preacher lays out all the ways things can go wrong, he identifies the way for making things go right and that is acknowledging God's Presence."

Looking at her father, Emma saw that he was fading. She said, "Before we call it a night, I've got to ask you about the Preacher's attitude toward women. I know I said earlier that I would need to do further thinking on this, but it would help to have your opinion. Was he a woman hater?"

The old man chuckled. "Your mother asked the same question. She was always torn when it came to Ecclesiastes. The proverbs and practical counsel had great appeal to her. The Preacher's view of women, not so much.

"Personally, I don't think he was a woman hater. In fact, he loved women … probably too much. I think his statement about not finding one good woman had more to do with his recognition that women were his Achilles' heel. Maybe what he was saying was that every woman was a trap for him, that he couldn't trust himself with any of them."

"If what you say is true, I find it troubling that he blamed the women for his problem. On the other hand, he certainly displayed a high regard for marriage and home," Emma responded. "I don't feel we've gotten to the bottom of this. I'll have to give this more thought."

Yawning, she stood up, walked over and kissed her father on the forehead. With a sweet smile, she said good night and headed for bed.

As the old man got ready for bed, he thought about how delighted Sarah would have been with the conversation tonight. While not a feminist, she'd had a clear sense of the value of womanhood. Her daughter's marriage had deeply troubled her, and she wouldn't have been unhappy to see Emma leave Gil. It would have been encouraging for her to hear Emma begin to get a little sense of outrage over someone's attitude toward women.

Like her daughter, her spirituality had been practical and demanded absolute honesty of heart. Theological debates had quickly bored her. She would rather have read a biography than a novel. Even in the Bible she preferred the stories of Ruth and Esther over the complexities of Paul.

He had often gone to Sarah with his ideas about Ecclesiastes. Her practical insights had kept his writing and preaching grounded in reality. During some of the darkest chapters of their lives, he knew she found great comfort in the words of the Preacher. His comments about time and chance in chapter nine had helped her cope with the senselessness of their son's death.

Looking in the mirror as he brushed his teeth, he felt a wave of grief wash over him. How he missed her. How he longed for her solid strength. She would have been a great writing partner. Why hadn't he written this book a decade ago? What was it Whittier had said? "Of all sad things of tongue or pen, the saddest are these, 'It might have been.'"

Tears blurred his vision as he turned out the light. Laying in bed one word pressed heavily on his chest … *meaningless.*

# CHAPTER 16

Since no one knows the future, who can tell
someone else what is to come. —Ecclesiastes 8:7

The next time Chris came in to work on the book,
he was surprised when, instead of pulling out
notes, his grandpa said he wanted to talk.

Chris sat down behind the desk. "What do you want
to talk about?"

"I've asked your mother to give me her perspective on
Ecclesiastes. What would you think about bringing her
into our discussions sometimes?"

His grandson thought a moment. "To be honest, I'm
not sure. Mom and I get along fine, but I'm not ready to
be totally open with her."

"I'm not sure that is the point. I doubt if you have been
totally open with me."

Chris's eyebrows shot up as he cocked his head. "Well,
I don't tell anyone everything, but I've been more open
with you than I have with anyone else."

"Thank you for that. All I ask is that you think about it. She and I are going to spend some time getting a middle-aged woman's perspective. I think her joining us could be helpful."

"Okay. I'll let you know."

The old man pulled his notes out from inside his lapboard. "Like we said last time, let's be a little more systematic."

They launched into a discussion about the structure of the book, and they ended an hour later with the agreement that Chris would write up their conclusions for his grandpa to review. Laptop in hand, he headed to his room.

The session had tired out the old man. In fact, there were several times when he'd felt a little lightheaded and lost focus. Maybe it was low blood sugar. He wasn't sure. He propped his lapboard on the floor against his chair and started to get up, but he couldn't. As he sat back, his vision began to narrow as if he were going to faint. Trying to raise his right arm to rub his eyes, he found that he couldn't move it. For a little while, it was as if there was no clear boundary between himself and his chair.

Eventually, his perceptions returned to normal. Glancing at the clock next to his bed, he realized twenty minutes had passed since Chris left the room. He wasn't sure what to do. He knew he'd had a mini-stroke and was sure it probably wasn't the first. Several times during the past few weeks, he'd felt a little lightheaded, but he'd written it off as hypoglycemia. This incident seemed much more serious, and he was scared.

When he tried to get up again, he was able to push himself to his feet. The amazing thing was that he felt fairly normal. He decided not to worry anyone but to talk to his doctor when he went in for his regular checkup next week. Walking unsteadily over to the bed, he lay down with the thought that a nap would do him good.

* * * * *

Back in his bedroom, Chris sat in the corduroy rocker. He thought about his mom and her involvement in the writing project.

Why he was hesitant was obvious. They hadn't talked about his personal life since he moved back home. He knew they were avoiding the trouble talking about it could bring. For him, it was less a fear of conflict than an unwillingness to disappoint.

Looking around his room, he realized how little had changed from when he'd lived at home. Besides the old posters, on one wall was a bookshelf that contained some of his more recent purchases. Many of the books, however, were from his childhood, ranging from the thin, large-format books from when he'd first started reading to Lemony Snicket. On top were two of the Star Wars Lego models he'd done as a child.

He thought about how he would approach this topic with his mom. Sitting at the kitchen table was probably the best. It wasn't very private, however. He didn't want to involve his grandpa in the conversation. Dealing with both of them at the same time wasn't a good idea. The weekend was coming up, and he determined to find a time when they could talk.

Having settled that in his mind, he decided to fix a sandwich before heading off to work. Seeing his grandpa's door ajar, he stepped over to ask whether Grandpa wanted him to fix him something. Hearing his heavy breathing, he quietly looked across the room at the prone figure with a sense of gratitude that they'd reconnected at this point in their lives. It was, he knew, a gift.

# CHAPTER 17

There is something else meaningless that
occurs on earth: the righteous who get what the
wicked deserve, and the wicked who get what
the righteous deserve. —Ecclesiastes 8:14

The old man spent the morning reviewing his notes and doing some writing on the role of proverbs in Ecclesiastes. He was trying to find anything to stay busy so he wouldn't think about the earlier episode. But in the quiet moments—and there were a lot of them each day—he imagined having another stroke, and it really scared him.

One recurring image was right out of a nightmare. He was sitting in his chair, and Emma came into his room and started telling him about her day. He moved his lips to reply, but nothing but gibberish came out. Just thinking about the image took his breath away. When that happened, his heart tripped so he couldn't tell whether it was skipping beats or getting ready to explode. He had to work hard to keep it from escalating into a panic attack.

Worse yet, he would imagine the same thing happening to him that had happened to his grandfather. He'd had a stroke one morning right after he got up. It felled him like he'd been cut down by an axe, and he lay next to his bed for ten hours, waiting for someone to come. By the time his son-in-law got there, he was humiliated that he'd relieved himself in his bedclothes.

Just being alone most of each weekday was beginning to scare him. His life had followed the well-worn path of so many of his generation. He'd left his parent's home to move into a college dorm. Marriage had come on the heels of graduation, and he and Sarah had been together over the next half century. Being alone, he decided, was a skill he hadn't yet developed, so he worked hard at keeping himself busy.

He was noodling with some ideas when Chris knocked on his door.

"Come in. I'm decent," the old man said with a chuckle. It struck him how many ways that simple phrase could be taken.

"What's so funny," Chris asked, smiling at his grandfather.

"I was trying to decode my invitation. Was I telling you I was properly clothed, or was there something Freudian going on about my character? I can hear this British voice in my head saying, 'I'm a decent sort of chap.'"

His grandson teased, "So how are we going to write this book on Ecclesiastes with that flight of fantasy?"

"I'm not sure about that, but don't we all have the creative gift?" he asked. "Some of us may nurture it more than others, but I have always thought that every night we all write a dozen short stories in our dreams. They may be bizarre, but they're ours nonetheless."

By now Chris was seated at the desk. His grandpa was always amazed by the casual cool he exuded. He was dressed in a rumpled, linen-colored cotton shirt and faded jeans. The cuff at the back of the left leg was frayed where it reached the floor beyond his sandals.

Before opening his laptop, Chris plunged in, "I'd like to talk about my ideas before I show you what I've been writing."

"Go for it," his grandpa said.

"I've been thinking about our last talk and how we can help a difficult book be interesting to the average reader."

"Good, because I talked with your mother a couple of days ago, and she kind of discouraged me. She said she would probably never pick up a book like the one we're working on."

"Well, I might have a way to deal with that. What if we stopped thinking about the structure of the book? I mean, that's like your English teacher forcing you to write an outline on your term paper or diagram a sentence. I think structure may be too artificial, and most people would find it boring. Your idea about the tapestry may be enough to help people work their way through it."

The old man gave a tentative nod in agreement.

"You've been telling me from the beginning that you wanted the book to be about life—to be real. And I think that's exactly what this is about. It isn't about how the Preacher organized the book but about how he addressed life. He was telling us that life is like yin and yang, beyond the sun and under the sun.

"And I think it goes even deeper than that. He wasn't just talking about complementary things like yin and yang. He was saying that life in a broken world is composed of some things that can't be reconciled. We don't just have light and darkness. We have good and bad, justice and injustice, life and death."

The old man thought about this for a minute and said, "So you're proposing that the Preacher didn't impose a structure on the book, life did and he wrote about it. Is that it?"

Chris nodded. "It isn't the Preacher who's bipolar. Life is." He paused. "Do you remember that mission trip I went on in high school to dig wells in Sarawak? I saw it there for the first time, even though I didn't realize it until I started helping you with the book."

His grandfather's "Hmmm" let Chris know he was with him.

"I thought of the trip as a lark. Here was a bunch of teenage guys staying in thatched huts in the middle of the jungle. We were exhilarated with the thought that we were living on the edge. You know adolescent males—we felt like we were killing a lion or performing some other rite of passage. Each night we went to sleep under our mosquito nets, listening to the sound of frogs so loud it was like a bamboo band serenading us to sleep. Each morning we awoke to the call of parrots and cockatoos and who knows what else whistling and popping and chirping. Occasionally we heard the *whoop-whoop* of howler monkeys talking to each other across the valley.

"We would wash up in a stream, cook our own food over a fire, and then walk up the trail from our hut to the longhouse, where we were digging the well. I can still feel the warmth of the morning sun and humidity so heavy you worked up a sweat just walking. The smell of the jungle was like something ripe and rich and loamy at the same time.

"Everyone in that village lived in one long structure with a single veranda across the front, kind of like English row houses. I had never seen anything like it. Pure subsistence living. They had nothing.

"But what I came to realize when we got to know them better was that they were happy in so many ways. Their families were intact. The little kids played under their homes, which were up on stilts, or out in the garden behind—teasing, running, but most of all, laughing and having fun, just like we did when we were kids."

"So how does this relate to the Preacher?"

"I'm not sure entirely," the young man replied. "I think it has more to do with life. In my adolescent mind, I had equated civilization and wealth with happiness, and it wasn't like that at all. We imagined we were going to do something that would pull them above their miserable lives. And we probably did with the well.

"We were surprised to find they were both poor and happy, hungry but satisfied with their lives. We were so smug until we discovered there was something they had that we wanted—a simplicity of life, a transparency of relationships we all longed for.

"When I put those experiences together with Ecclesiastes, I realized the Preacher was trying to break free from the way everyone in his day looked at life—to see it not just from a different perspective but for what it really was. And so he wrote his book to help us see life with an honesty of heart and a transparency of soul so we could know what is really important. I think he would have liked those villagers.

"I'm probably romanticizing them now, but it's like they existed on the lowest level of Maslow's hierarchy of need—you know, safety and all of that. And yet in so many important ways they were really living. I'm not saying they were self-actualized. I'm just saying they were sucking the marrow out of life and eating the bones."

The old man thought about this a minute. "May I read what you've written?"

Chris handed his grandfather a sheaf of papers and said, "So let me set this up for you. This will follow the chapter that introduces the book as a tapestry."

"Okay."

Laying the stack of papers on his lapboard, the old man began to read. He paused several times to stare off into space and then returned to reading. After the third page, he looked up at his grandson, who had begun surfing the Internet on his computer, and said, "I like the link you've made with paradox in the rest of the Bible. I think you're onto something there." He began to read aloud.

> Isn't that why the Bible used so many paradoxes? Love your life and lose it. Lose your life and find it. The first last and last first. Forget you came from dust and to dust you will return.
>
> So why couldn't a whole book of the Bible embrace paradox and live with contradiction?

Too often we want the neat package, the Hollywood ending. We want to know the answer to every question. But the Bible uses paradox because human language and understanding are too limited to encompass the truth about life. Ecclesiastes is in the Bible because the Preacher knew someone had to tell us it wasn't that simple or clear or easy.

The old man read on for a while longer, put down the papers, and said, "I like it. It expresses your ideas very well. Let me see what spin I would put on this."

# CHAPTER 18

Then I saw all that God has done. No one can
comprehend what goes on under the sun.
—Ecclesiastes 8:17

*E*mma felt that the tension had been building toward
this evening for weeks. Earlier that day Chris asked
whether they might talk after supper. Like a computer
stuck in an endless loop, her mind had been churning
on his request ever since. She could almost hear the
hard drive grinding away, unable to break out and do
meaningful work. When the last dish was put away, Chris
sat in his place at the table while his mother finished
wiping the counters. Emma came over, drying her hands
on a dishtowel, and sat in her chair.

Quiet domestic sounds surrounded them—the hum
and thrum of the dishwasher, the thumping of the dryer
in the distance, ice dropping into the icemaker in the
door of the refrigerator. Each sound was comforting in its
own way to Emma. They represented an important part
of the person she had been for a long time. She knew the

word *husband* meant "house-band." That function had been gone a long time before Gil left.

What Emma did know was that she was the glue of the family. She knew that good husbands, like her dad, provided security and boundaries for the home. But for her and her family, she was the one who held them together. The few times she'd been gone overnight to conferences when the kids were teenagers, she'd known the home became a motel as soon as she stepped out the door. They ate what they wanted and when they wanted. Conversations between the siblings and their father were cursory at best and monosyllabic at worst. Her return always came as a relief to everyone, not just because of the better meals and clean clothes, but because her cords of love drew everyone back together again.

And so tonight Emma and her adult son sat quietly preparing for what she knew was a very important conversation.

Chris cleared his throat and shifted in his seat before he spoke.

"Mom, I know you're aware of some big changes have been happening in my life. I'm sorry it has taken me so long to tell you what is going on, but I needed time to sort it out for myself before I talked with you."

"I understand," Emma said. "I knew we would talk when you were ready. It was tolerable only because I knew you and your grandpa were spending time together."

"Thanks for making that happen. It's really been fun helping him. We've had some good talks. I think he's doing better emotionally, though he spaces out sometimes when we're working, and I'm not sure what to make of that."

"Let's both keep an eye on him and let the other know if we notice anything. I don't think he would tell us if something was going on."

Emma thought of her father blissfully asleep in the next room. She'd hoped for a number of years that Chris was going to walk in his footsteps. Now, she suspected, she was going to hear otherwise.

Chris spoke. "I need to confirm what you've probably already guessed. This whole thing with Dad has ended up being the final straw in my relationship with God. I'm sorry. I know what your faith means to you and the dreams you had for me. I just can't do it anymore."

Emma stood up and asked, "I'm going to brew some tea. Would you like something?"

"I'm good."

When she walked over to the stove and started heating water. Chris got up and joined her. As she puttered around between the stove and the sink, he leaned back against the counter.

He continued, "One thing I don't want you doing is blaming yourself."

"It's too late for that," she confessed. *If he only knew*, she said to herself.

"You need to know I don't hold you responsible for any of what went on. You have always been there for me, and I really respect how you've survived all this. You deserve better."

As she smiled, a tear slipped unashamedly down her cheek. She reached up and brushed back a lock of hair from his forehead. "I don't feel blameless or noble or strong. In fact, most of the time I'm pretty much a mess."

Pouring the hot water into her mug, Emma returned to the table with the cup in one hand and a tea bag in the other. She sat down, and Chris followed her.

"I wish I could lighten your load instead of increasing it," he said. "I know you've been worrying about me since I came home."

"Just like you've been worried about me – that's what love does." She reached over and laid her hand on his.

Now that the worst was out, Emma relaxed a little. She picked up the tea bag and dipped up and down while what she had heard slowly steeped in her mind.

Finally she said, "So is there anything I can do to help?"

"I'm not sure. At the risk of sounding like Albert Einstein, what I need is space and time. I just need you to continue to respect the journey I'm on."

"I do worry about you staying out so late. I'm not trying to lay a guilt trip on you, but until you get home at night, no matter how late it is, I really can't get to sleep."

Chris paused. "I'm sorry about that. I didn't know. Would it help if I called or texted you to let you know I'll be late?"

"You're twenty-five years old. I can't expect that of you."

"I know. But I'm offering it to you."

"Then I'll take it. It might help."

"One other thing," Chris said. "Why don't you join Grandpa and me when you can? That way you will be part of the conversation. I don't like the fact that you've been carved out."

"I haven't felt like that, but I will accept your invitation."

Chris stood up, stretched, and yawned. "Thanks for understanding."

"You knew I would," Emma said with a smile.

"Yeah, I did." He paused a moment, reached down, and pulled his mom to her feet, wrapping his arms around her. Her soft hair tickled his nose as he kissed the top of her head. She squeezed back and thought how nice it was to be held by someone who loved her.

"I love you, Mom."

"I love you too, Son."

Turning out the lights they retired to their rooms.

# CHAPTER 19

So I reflected on all this and concluded that
the righteous and the wise and what they do
are in God's hands, but no one knows whether
love or hate awaits them. —Ecclesiastes 9:1

*H*is was a generation that dressed up to go out.
When he and Sarah flew, both wore what the
business community called "dressy casual." Today he was
going out and had on his black wing tips, a pair of dark-
blue dress pants, and a white button-down oxford cloth
shirt. His tweed sport coat was hanging in his closet,
waiting to finish the ensemble. Ties were something he'd
quit when he retired.

Two big events were happening today. The first was
Emma's 10 o'clock appointment with her lawyer. The
second was his visit to the doctor. Emma had taken a
personal day since she was involved in both.

He was already dressed and at breakfast, even though
his appointment wasn't until one thirty. Emma, sitting
across the table from him, was dressed in a dark-gray

pantsuit and white blouse with one-inch black heels. He noticed again how much she looked like her mother at that age.

They were talking about Joel, his son, her brother. He was someone rarely discussed because it was like an old and painful chapter he had a hard time making himself go back and read. The topic had come up because of Emma's trip to the lawyer. She was finalizing papers in response to Gil's request for the formal "dissolution" of the marriage. She had to submit them within twenty days of being served. Her financial profile also had to be presented to the court.

"I'm glad Gil is looking for an easy out so he can marry that woman," Emma said. The old man could hear the anger and pain as Emma spoke of her.

"I wonder how she feels, having broken up a marriage," she said.

"Are you sure it was her fault?"

Emma looked up sharply at her father. Her body sagged after a moment. "I guess she hasn't broken anything up. She just happened to be there when things fell apart."

The old man could see this insight was a painful one for his daughter. It was easier to blame an outsider than to face the cruel fact that your husband didn't love you anymore. He was sympathetic with her ploy.

"At least he only wants his tools and half the house. He already won my heart and then broke it. I can't stand the thought that he might win in this as well."

When she'd told her father earlier that week that her only choice was to sell the house, he'd offered to buy Gil's half. He said, "You and your kids are all I have left.

All my eggs are, in fact, in one basket." It was a simple statement of the obvious. When his son had died twenty years earlier, the potential for a large family had been thwarted.

"How did you and mom survive all of that?" Emma had asked.

"Survive is probably a good word because healing, closure, and other terms are woefully inadequate. Basically we just hung on to each other for dear life. Once he was gone, the finality of changing our will to leave everything to you was one of the most difficult things we had to do other than bury him."

Sitting at the breakfast table that morning, the old man reassured his daughter that he couldn't think of anything he would rather do with his money. It would certainly be of more value to him in her home than in the bank.

She reluctantly nodded in agreement.

As she finished her cup of tea, she said, "I still miss him, you know."

He quietly looked at her with sad eyes.

She said, "I know we were very different and didn't agree on much. But I did love him. I think I was jealous of him and all the attention he always drew. In his presence I was always a wallflower. I don't think he wished that on me. That was just the response of the world to him. He was someone very special."

Her father observed, "Your mother and I grieved so differently. She raged at God, at life, at me for some unnamed oversight. I, on the other hand, buried the grief deep inside only to be taken out in safe and quiet moments.

I literally worked my way through it. Unfortunately that commitment to work made me that much less available to your mom.

"She, on the other hand, needed to talk and cry her way out. Fortunately, our love for each other and faith in God weren't shaken, at least not permanently. In the end I think both relationships were stronger for having weathered the storm."

Emma thought a minute and said, "I don't know how you did it. If something happened to Chris, I could never forgive myself or God." She paused. "And certainly not Gil."

"I don't think any of us know ahead of time what we would do," the old man said. "Most of us have no idea how strong we really are until we're faced with a crisis. Most get through it."

Both of them stood and took their dishes to the sink. Emma went into the office to check her briefcase to make sure she had all the paperwork needed. Walking back through the kitchen, she gave her father a peck on the cheek and told him she thought she would be home a little before lunch.

As the sound of her car faded, the old man walked quietly back into his room and sat down in his chair. He closed his eyes and leaned his head back on the soft leather. Reflecting on their conversation, the old man thought about those events so long ago and yet so fresh. When he looked back from this distance, certain aspects rose above the fog of pain and regret and stood out as clear as the Tetons on a spring day. One was that this was a kid who had it all. The old man couldn't think of one area where his son hadn't excelled.

Then there was his penchant for risk. Joel had gotten into springboard diving in high school and then motocross. Within six months of getting his license, he had three speeding tickets. The old man's insurance company had threatened to cancel their policy.

Unfortunately, the risk-taking began to take on some of the qualities of the Preacher's experiment. Joel seemed to have determined he was going to try whatever was out there. And for what reason, his father wasn't sure. He didn't think it was to find the meaning of life. Maybe it was to avoid thinking about it.

He and his son were so different. Sarah was always grateful that there were no love children out there, nor had he done anything at that point to permanently damage his future.

After law school, Joel got married, and for a year or so it seemed as if all was going to work out. Then one day his wife came home and said she was leaving him, which she did within a week. That first big failure in life had made something snap in him, and his risky behavior came back with a vengeance. It was only a matter of time before they got the call in the middle of the night saying he had crashed his car and hadn't survived.

If he was honest with himself, Emma's divorce and Chris's drinking resonated too much with those events from the past. In the bleak hours of the night, he feared they might head down the same path. He literally hoped to God that the Preacher was wrong on this and that his family wasn't caught in a meaningless cycle of destructive behavior. He hoped for something new under the sun.

As he pushed all that out of his mind, there were two immediate things he needed to sort out. One was what to tell the doctor and the other was what to tell his family.

When Emma got back at eleven thirty, there was a joyless relief in her voice. "Well, that's pretty much over. My lawyer said this can all be wrapped up in a short time once the title is transferred and the money changes hands."

"I'm glad," her father said.

After lunch he went back into his room and returned, wearing his sport coat. In spite of the toll of time, he thought he still cut quite a dapper figure. He was looking forward to getting out of the house, even if it was just to go to a doctor's appointment.

Three hours later they were back, and the old man went quietly to his room, took off his coat, and hung it up. The thought flitted through his mind that he would rather be buried in that than in his black preacher suit. It was less dignified but more him. He collapsed into his chair rather than sitting down in it. It felt like the spinning of his thoughts might create enough centrifugal force to throw all the important things in his life out of their orbit. The news he'd gotten wasn't disastrous. It was just ominous.

On the ride back home, he'd largely been silent, responding to Emma's questions about his visit by saying only that he needed to think about a few things.

That night over supper Emma tried to get her father to talk about what his doctor had told him. By now four hours had passed since they'd left the doctor's office, and her anxiety was mounting that whatever had transpired between her dad and his physician hadn't been good.

"Okay, Dad. Out with it. I can't stand not knowing." Her voice carried notes of both desperation and urgency.

The old man sat quietly for a minute, took a deep breath, and said, "Over the past several weeks I've had what the doctor calls TIAs. Mini-strokes. No permanent damage, just little harbingers of bigger things that might come. They did a Doppler ultrasound of my carotids and believe there is a narrowing that is the likely source of the trouble.

"She feels I have a pretty healthy diet, so she wants me to start on an aspirin regimen and see her in a month. In the meantime I need to keep track of any strange sensations and call 9-1-1 if there are any further symptoms."

"So are you a ticking time bomb?" his daughter asked.

"Something like that, I guess. About a third of those with TIAs end up with a stroke. And then all bets are off." He sat there, thinking, *Just when things were starting to progress. My living circumstances, my grieving, my book.* Since the doctor had delivered the verdict, his arms and legs felt as though he had to command them to move. A numbness had settled in his brain, too. It wasn't that he couldn't think. It was that he didn't want to.

"I'm sorry, sweetie. I know you just lost your mother, and now it seems like I'm next in line." He paused to marshal his resolve. "I promise you two things. One, I don't want to die. And two, I will do everything I can so that won't happen."

He smiled with an attempt at being reassuring.

Emma looked down at her hands folded in front of her on the kitchen table. Laced together like that, they looked like praying hands. "I'm with you every step of the way," She sighed. "Just promise you won't hide anything from me. I'm going to have a hard enough time not worrying when I'm at work. I have to know that you won't hide anything."

She said this while looking him straight in the eye and with a conviction that left no doubt in his mind how she felt.

"I promise," he said. "And I will talk with Chris the first chance I get."

After a minute's silence, he said he was tired and thought he would head for bed. His daughter got up and walked around the table to where he was sitting. Standing behind his chair, she bent, wrapped her arms around his shoulders, and laid her head next to his. Crossing his arms, he reached up and held hers, soaking in the love and care as if his life depended on them. And maybe it did.

# CHAPTER 20

Whatever your hand finds to do, do it with
all your might. —Ecclesiastes 9:9

*A* week passed since the doctor's visit. The old
man talked with his grandson about the TIAs.
Chris's concern was as strong as his mom's. He resolved
to put more work in on the book in case their time was
shorter than he'd initially thought.

His grandfather seemed more determined than ever
to complete his work on the project.

The previous day he had given Emma and Chris the
assignment to read through chapter three of Ecclesiastes
so they could talk about it the next day.

Since Chris didn't have to be to work until one o'clock,
the three of them enjoyed a waffle breakfast and then met
in the old man's room. Chris sat in his usual place at
the small desk, his mom brought in her chair from the
kitchen, and the old man was seated in the leather chair
with his lapboard and Bible.

He began by setting up where he wanted them to go. "Chris, I know what you said about not worrying about the organization of the book, but I want to introduce chapter three by putting it in context. Some of this is territory we have covered before, but bear with me.

"In chapter one the Preacher says he wants to know what will give life meaning. He asks, 'What are we to do with our lives under the sun?' Then, using a short poem, he outlines the contributing themes concerning remembrance versus no remembrance, meaning versus meaninglessness, and satisfaction versus no satisfaction. He will come back to these themes over and over again in the book.

"Once his themes are laid out in chapter one, he tells us in chapter two about the experiment he conducted to discover the things people have done to give meaning to their lives. He tries work, possessions, and pleasure. In the end, he says it is all *hevel*.

"Emma," he said with a little tip of his head toward his grandson, "here is where Chris and I disagree a little bit. He feels the Preacher is saying *hevel* is 'meaninglessness.' I propose he is saying that no matter what we do, we will be living in a fog, unable to fully understand the meaning of life. Are you with me so far?"

His daughter and grandson nodded.

He continued, "As we move to the end of chapter two, we find the first apparent contradiction. After telling us work and pleasure and possessions are *hevel*, he ends the chapter stating that these very things are gifts of God."

He paused to see whether either had a comment. When they didn't, he proceeded. "What I see in chapter two, starting in verse twenty-four, is the beginning of the first counterpoint to *hevel*. It will run all the way through the end of chapter three. And as I think we have all agreed, you can trace this back-and-forth pattern, the dialectic, through the rest of the book."

As he paused again and got no response, he began to suspect that he was being coddled. They were going noble on him to help him accomplish his dream before it was too late.

"Okay, guys, I appreciate you being unpaid ambassadors from the Make-A-Wish Foundation, but not much is going to be accomplished if you're playing nice with the old man because he might kick the bucket."

That brought a murmur of protest from both Emma and Chris.

"Daddy," Emma said, "we're just trying to be helpful."

"I can use a little less help and a little more argument," the old man said.

Without waiting for a response, he threw out his first question. "So if I'm right and these couplets that begin chapter three are part of the positive counterpoint, how can we say dying as well as birth, weeping as well as laughter, and war as well as peace are part of God's plan? Or, as it says in verse eleven, 'He has made everything beautiful in its time.' Really?"

Emma was the first to speak. "I was thinking about this when I read the book the other night. The only thing I could figure is that it's saying God made the possibility of these things, but when they occur is up to us. So their ability to bring beauty to our lives is up to us."

After a moment's hesitation, Chris said, "Okay, I'm going out on a limb here with the two of you, but I'm going to speak, ignoring verse eleven and what it might say about God's plan. I think the couplets are like the phrase we hear all the time: 'Timing is everything.' Birth isn't always a beautiful thing if it's a miscarriage or the result of rape. War isn't always a bad thing. Ask the British if they wanted the 'Peace in our time' of Neville Chamberlain or the 'Blood, toil, tears, and sweat' of Churchill. I think it's a statement of the obvious and that there are few if any things that are always right or always wrong, even the couplet about love and hate. I could love evil and inflicting pain, or I could hate evil and hate the pain inflicted on someone I love."

A thoughtful silence filled the room, which the old man finally broke. "So is there really any difference between what the two of you said? Is it just an observation about life that doesn't require a God to make it so?"

Chris responded, "I think this is a case of it depending on your presuppositions. I'm presupposing that there is no God, and I can come to a very similar conclusion as Mom, who assumes there is a God."

"Or perhaps you're describing a third option," his grandfather said. "What if it's proof neither for nor against the existence of God? Chris, you and I have agreed that the Preacher is giving us a picture of life. Perhaps this poem is just an observation about life. It certainly doesn't imply that God is manipulating these things to make them beautiful. They just are if they are done in season."

Emma spoke next. "Dad, I see what you're saying, but I think that can only be true if we take the poem out of context. The Preacher just told us in chapter two that food and family and work are gifts of God and that there is a deeper level to the things of life. What does he say?"

With this she picked up her Bible and turned to chapter three and read, "'There is a time for everything, and a season for every activity under the heavens.' Then he ends with the haunting phrase: 'He has made everything beautiful in its time.' It's hard for me to buy that he doesn't intend to put God at the center or perhaps behind all of this."

"Something just occurred to me," her father said. "The Preacher's picture of God in the book is more as provider than intervener. I can't remember him talking about prayer, though he does refer to making vows to God in chapter five. Several times he says it is God who makes things straight or crooked, but he doesn't propose those initial conditions can be changed. For the most part, however, He is a provider. He has provided the structure of the world and apparently the laws that govern relationships. And it seems that the more one fits harmoniously into that structure, the more one will have a chance to experience the beauty of life."

Chris weighed in. "This is where I have the problem with God in Ecclesiastes. The Preacher speaks of injustice, but he neither prays for justice nor has God making things right. Look at verse 16. 'And I saw something else under the sun: In the place of judgment—wickedness was there, in the place of justice—wickedness was there.'"

"But you stopped too soon," said the old man. "Right here in the next verse he talks about judgment. 'I said to myself, "God will bring into judgment both the righteous and the wicked, for there will be a time for every activity, a time to judge every deed.'"

The old man went on, "Maybe this is part of the time and season thing mentioned earlier. Under the sun mankind should view the good things in life as gifts of God. Under the sun even the normal birth and death have a season and we, in our free will, should try to figure out when they will be a blessing.

"But above the sun, God also has seasons—in this case the season of judgment when accounts will be settled. You're right, Chris. The Preacher doesn't see God intervening in this life very much, but he does believe God settles accounts."

Emma chimed in. "So where does the verse on eternity fit into all of this?"

"Let me read all of verse eleven," Chris volunteered. "'He has made everything beautiful in its time. He has also set eternity in the human heart; yet no one can fathom what God has done from beginning to end.' Grandpa has spent more time with this than I have, but this seems to be one of the great mysteries in the book. I don't think there is much agreement among the scholars on this."

The old man said, "You're right, Chris. Translations range from 'eternity' to 'the world' to 'toil.' And this brings up a major issue in writing our book. How do we deal honestly with these tough verses and various translations?

"For me, everything in this verse depends on context. Look at the three points the Preacher is making. One, everything is beautiful or appropriate in its time. Two, He has put something in man's heart. And three, no one understands the work of God from the beginning to the end. One and three have to do with time. Why wouldn't number two? I think eternity fits the best. The same word is used in verse fourteen and is translated as 'forever.'

"I think the Preacher brings this as a counterpoint to *hevel* in the first two chapters by saying God has given us some extraordinary, ordinary gifts in these couplets," the old man said. "They are ordinary in that they are available to everyone all of the time. They are extraordinary when used at their appropriate times. But—and here's the kicker—we will never figure it all out. God has put within mankind's heart the desire to see the big picture, but only He can really do that."

"But, Dad," said Emma, "that begs an important question. Why would God put something in our hearts that will never be satisfied?"

She looked back and forth between her son and father. The question was obviously one they hadn't thought of before.

When they didn't speak, Emma said, "Here's what I think. God has never given us a desire which He did not provide the ability and resources to satisfy. From the beginning he gave us taste buds and food that would be satisfying. He gave us sex and the partners to meet that need. So what does this mean concerning our desire for eternity? Is it a desire that can be satisfied?" Again, she paused waiting for an answer.

She continued, "I can think of two parts to the answer. One, the desire itself for something bigger and fuller and higher is very different than our other desires. They are so earthbound, so mundane."

At this point her father jumped in. "Maybe it has to do with our desire for meaning. Something can't be considered meaningless unless there is a possibility for meaning. That is what the Preacher's experiment was all about. Finding meaning."

Chris had been hesitant to enter the God-talk discussion. Now he said, "I read a book on philosophy once that spoke of pragmatic idealism. The basic idea is that an individual holds a set of ideals he or she knows are unreachable. However, rather than abandoning them because of that, they become the target toward which one aims. The goal is to always be moving in the direction of the ideal, even after conceding it can never be reached. Maybe the Preacher was a pragmatic idealist."

"Let me share my second point," Emma said. "I was surprised to not find anything about heaven in Ecclesiastes, only eternity. I have thought about that and have decided that there is a clear implication that heaven had to have been real for the Preacher. Why else would there be a judgment? Doesn't he say at the end of the book that God will bring everything into judgment? If there is no reward or punishment, why would it matter if there is a settling of accounts?"

"So following your line of reasoning," her father said, "eternity has been put in our hearts both as an ideal for life under the sun and as a hope for something beyond the sun."

"I hate to be a spoiler in this," Chris said, "but I'm going to have to start getting ready for work pretty soon."

"Okay," said the old man. "I'm kind of wearing down as well." He paused before going on, "Not wanting to drag this out, but here is something that just occurred to me. Maybe this poem in chapter three is the counterpoint to the poem in chapter one. The first one talked about the meaningless cycles and futilities of life under the sun. Here is a poetic counterpoint that says, yes, there are some things like birth and death that happen over and over. But they don't have to be meaningless or futile. They can be satisfying if they happen in their season."

Closing their Bibles, Chris and Emma stood and said their good-byes.

Remaining in his chair, the old man reflected back on the morning. He couldn't remember a time when he'd enjoyed himself more—even if they were coddling him. The whole discussion rose far above his passion for writing a book. Here was the real value of the Preacher's words—a touching of hearts and minds about essentials.

He laid his head back on the chair, closed his eyes, and drifted off to sleep.

# CHAPTER 21

The race is not to the swift, or the battle to the strong, nor does food come to the wise or wealth to the brilliant or favor to the learned; but time and chance happen to them all. —Ecclesiastes 9:11

That evening at supper Emma asked her father how he felt about the morning session.

"It would be hard for me to put into words how much I enjoyed it," he said, choking up a little bit. "What about you?"

Emma started to say she was glad to have been part of something important to the men in her life. Then she caught herself and thought *I can't go through the rest of my life thinking like this. What did the morning mean to me? What did I get out of it?* It startled her to realize she didn't know.

Without answering her father's question, she got up and started to clear the table. As she set her plate on the counter, she heard the clatter of silverware on the oak table. Turning, she saw her father slump in his chair.

"Daddy!" she screamed as she ran to his side. She caught him as he began a slow motion tip sideways. It took all her strength to lower him onto the braided rug. Putting a hand on either side of his face, she looked into his eyes, but he didn't seem to be aware of anything around him.

With a frightened edge to her voice, she shouted, "Daddy, can you hear me?" Leaning down, she put her ear next to his mouth and could feel the light puff of his shallow breathing. Pulling her cell phone out of her pocket, she tried to dial 9-1-1. Her hands were shaking so badly that she couldn't hit the right keys on the touchpad. Twice she almost dropped the phone.

"Why do they make these things so slippery?" she said as panic began to rise in her throat.

Muttering to herself, "Come on, come on," she tried three times before she dialed the number.

"9-1-1 operator, how may I help you?" a calm female voice said in her ear.

"I think my father has had a stroke."

The call lasted only a minute, but she was able to tell the operator where they lived and was told in return to continue monitoring his breathing and heart rate.

"Don't you die on me, do you hear me?" she cried in desperation as she knelt by the inert, beloved figure before her. Holding his right hand in both of hers, she was aware of nothing outside the drama playing out on her kitchen floor. Tears flowed unchecked down her cheeks and dropped unnoticed onto her father's blue V-neck sweater.

"Our Father," she said several times. *Why can't I remember the rest of the prayer,* she thought. And then something clicked inside her. She blinked and saw a fork partially hidden underneath her father's left arm. There were several peas scattered on the floor beyond that.

She took a deep breath and said, "Daddy's had a stroke," as if realizing it consciously for the first time. Picking up her phone where she'd dropped it, she called Chris at work.

When he answered, she said, "Grandpa's had a stroke. I called 9-1-1, and they're on their way."

"Is he okay?" Chris asked. "I mean, is he breathing?"

"He's breathing, and his pulse is steady. Listen, I hear the siren. Meet me at the hospital." She hung up and ran to the front door as the ambulance pulled into the driveway. *They're so young*, she thought as the EMTs came up the steps.

"He's in the kitchen," she said, pointing down the hallway. She watched as they took his vitals, talking quietly to him the whole time. Her hands were still trembling. In what seemed like only a moment, they had him on the stretcher and were wheeling him out the door. She followed close behind.

"Ma'am," said the dark-haired one. "Why don't you follow us in your car. Are you going to be able to drive okay?"

"I'm fine."

Returning to the house, she grabbed her purse and keys and ran to her car.

\* \* \* \* \*

A series of flashbulb memories were etched in Emma's mind from the next first few days: her father slowly tipping out of his chair; his unresponsive, uncomprehending form lying on the kitchen floor; his waking up in the hospital and looking old and frail; the first squeeze of his left hand on hers; Chris asleep in the chair next to his hospital bed.

They took turns at the hospital, and it wasn't until the end of the week that she and her son were able to sit at the kitchen table and talk one evening. She was exhausted and knew he felt the same way. For what seemed like the hundredth time that week, she thought about how quickly life can change. In a split second, she could have lost her father. There were so many contingencies. What if she hadn't been home, or what if the incident had happened in the middle of the night? What if they had lived in the country? *Was it all time and chance?* she wondered.

The thought of losing him and being alone again immobilized her diaphragm, making it hard to breathe. Unwelcome or not, she was beginning to believe that was going to be her lot in life. Would she be able to handle it? Chris's voice pulled her back to the present.

"Did the doctor say when he'd be coming home?"

"She said he would probably be out of the hospital by Sunday. He may not need to go to rehab since they were able to get the clot buster into him so soon after he had the stroke. If he needs it, they will send home health. If he's in a wheelchair, we'll need to put in a ramp to get him in and out of the house. I know that's a lot of ifs."

"There's some wood in the garage. I can make the ramp if I need to," Chris responded. "How did he seem today?"

"Distant. Depressed. Kind of apathetic. I'm not sure, but I think that's pretty normal for a stroke victim. Let me reword that, for someone who has had a stroke. His mind seems to be clearing, but he is still having a little trouble forming his words."

"So what's the long-term prognosis?" Chris asked.

"I think it's too early to tell. Apparently the first six weeks are critical. The doctor seems optimistic that he'll recover his speech. Time will tell on the use of his right arm and leg."

"How can I help?"

She thought a minute and then said, "I'm not sure. Right now I think our presence is what he needs. In the long run, a lot will depend on his will to fight."

"I will call Kristen with an update before I go to bed," she added.

* * * * *

In his room Chris lay on his bed, thinking about his grandfather. It didn't seem fair that this would happen just when they were adjusting to the new normal. He felt the old anger rising in his chest as he thought about his grandfather lying in the hospital. He knew why he was angry. Who he was angry at still troubled him.

The next morning, when he was alone in the house, he slipped into his grandfather's bedroom. Sitting in the old leather chair, he looked around. It was the first time he had gone into the room without his grandfather there. Now he had time to really look at the little world his grandfather had created for himself in the only space he could call his own.

He got up and walked over to the bookshelf. On top he saw a picture of his grandma and grandpa taken years before; they were standing inside the burned-out shell of the old Coventry Cathedral. They were holding hands and looking youthful and energetic. He figured they were younger in that picture than his mom was now.

And then there were his books. Looking at the titles and pulling some of them off the shelf told him of his grandfather's interests beyond Ecclesiastes. There were a number of books on psychology and philosophy. He liked history, especially the Civil War and Lincoln. One whole shelf was taken up with books on creation and evolution. What surprised him was the number of mysteries. Some authors he knew, such as Agatha Christie and P. D. James. But others he had never heard of, such as Ruth Rendell and Ngaio Marsh. What it was about these authors, he wondered, that his grandfather loved? He suspected that each of the shelves represented a mystery to be solved, whether it was something as obvious as a detective novel or as sublime as Ecclesiastes.

Looking around the room, he saw a linoleum block with the face of an old, bearded man carved in it. He suspected his grandfather had carved it and had not had a print made. Apparently he liked the look of the block and had it framed and hung it on the wall. On top of the nightstand was a sketch pad. He opened it and found some well-done drawings, mostly still life images and landscapes.

In the far corner was an old two-drawer file cabinet. Pulling open the top drawer, he saw manila folders filled with notes on Ecclesiastes. The second drawer contained handwritten sermon outlines. A quick glance told him his grandfather apparently kept every talk he'd ever given.

Sitting back down and looking around, Chris was struck by the thought that he was seeing the distilled remnants of a whole life. Here were those things deemed worthy of preserving and displaying. He figured each object represented something or someone important in his grandfather's life. Each was likely a cue for a memory of something cherished.

The overall impression, he realized, was that of decay. The books were old, some already starting to fall apart. The paper in the file folders was turning yellow, and the pencil marks were fading. In fact, nothing of his grandfather's was new. He wasn't sure, but it looked like all of it dated to a time twenty or more years ago.

His mind played down the years. After his grandfather died, his mother would inherit these things. She would probably keep some and give some to her kids who might or might not keep them. He imagined that by the next generation little of what was here would survive. If it didn't disintegrate on its own, the intrinsic value it had today would likely be gone. And then someone would ask, "Why keep it?"

*Within two generations from today*, he thought, *all evidence of Grandpa's life will be gone.* Only a headstone and the DNA he'd passed along in his genes would remain. Deep within his own heart Chris knew the same number of generations would result in a similar dissolution of his life.

With his grandfather in the hospital and the impact it was having on him, he knew he had to guard against becoming overly sentimental. However, sitting in that worn leather chair with the dusky smell of old books and the artifacts of a long life viewed in the yellow light of the sun filtered through the curtains, he thought he understood for the first time his grandfather's fascination with the words of the Preacher. Maybe he was right in thinking it was the fleeting nature of life that made it *hevel*.

# CHAPTER 22

As fish caught in a cruel net, or birds taken by a
snare, so people are trapped by evil times that fall
unexpectedly on them. —Ecclesiastes 9:12

It was two o'clock before they got home from the hospital. Emma had left the house by nine thirty to check her father out. She knew from previous visits that the process could take hours, and it had. Her father had been quiet through most of the proceedings, talking only when asked a question. Emma wasn't sure whether he was embarrassed or depressed.

Her own feelings were a mix of relief and sadness. Being back at the hospital so soon after her mother's death had made her feel as if they were following the same trajectory for her father. When he'd moved in a couple of months ago, grief had incapacitated him. This was a whole different story. As a mother, she knew it was natural to imagine the worst for those she loved. Her fears this time didn't feel like the product of her imagination.

Emma knew he could get along fairly well with a walker, but his right side was still weak. His leg would sometimes buckle without warning. When that happened, his right arm had a difficult time stabilizing himself. The physical therapist told them it might take another week or so before he could use the walker with confidence.

Unloading the wheelchair from the back of her car, Emma brought it around to the passenger door, helped her father make the transition, and wheeled him up the ramp Chris had made the day before and into the house. She chuckled when both of them let out audible sighs of relief when they got the wheelchair settled by the kitchen table.

"I'm going to make myself a cup of tea," Emma said. "Do you want anything?"

Her father thought a minute and said with deliberateness, "Piece of toast, glass of milk."

Someone who didn't know him might not have noticed. But the effort he made to speak pained Emma. This wasn't the golden-tongued orator who had been her father up until now. She realized her sadness had more to do with how she imagined he must be feeling about it. Every time he spoke, she had to resist the urge to help him find the right word or finish the sentence.

When the toast popped, she buttered it, spread honey on it, and brought it to the table with a glass of milk. She noticed he had already trained himself to use his left hand.

"Good," he gurgled through a half-full mouth.

Emma was glad for the silence—she sipping her tea and her father slowly working his way through his snack. She noticed he had some crumbs on the right side of his mouth and wondered whether there was still a lack of feeling on that side of his face.

"Think I'll take a nap," the old man said when he was done. Using both hands, he pushed back from the table. Emma watched as he struggled to turn the chair around using his stronger left arm and leg. She saw him trying to use his right arm but with little success. The chair veered from side to side as he compensated for his weak side.

"Do you want some help?" she asked.

"Let me see what I can do," he responded. It was painful to watch, but Emma took it as a good sign that he wanted to strengthen himself and improve. She cleared the table so she wouldn't have to observe the struggle.

"Let me know if you need help getting into bed."

He nodded, focusing on the effort to negotiate the door into his room. Once there he positioned the chair next to the bed and, using his stronger left arm, was able to stand and swing his backside onto the bed. Getting his left leg up on the bed was an effort that caused him to puff with the exertion. His right leg dangled over the side of the bed at the knee.

From her vantage point at the kitchen sink, Emma asked, "Would you like your shoes off?" He said yes and she came in, lifted his right leg into place, and took off his shoes.

"How about a light blanket?"

Again he nodded.

She got a summer blanket from the linen closet and spread it over him. She leaned down and kissed his forehead. She laughed as she wiped the perspiration off her lips.

"You burned a few calories doing that didn't you?"

He smiled and said, "Good to be home." Then he closed his eyes.

Emma made sure the wheelchair was in position and then quietly left the room, shutting the door.

\* \* \* \* \*

When he awoke two hours later, he felt as if he'd slept the sleep of the dead, though he thought he remembered hearing his door open and close a couple of times. He stared at the ceiling and realized that was what he'd been doing every day for almost a week. But this was different. It was his ceiling and his bed. He could smell his books, and everywhere he cast his eyes, he saw the anchor points of his life.

The past week had been the nightmare he feared. At first he thought he was going to die. With time he realized he might just be disabled. For him, that was worse, especially when he couldn't speak at all. Now, at least, he had hope. He could speak, and with effort he believed it would continue to improve. Truthfully, he wouldn't have been that upset if he'd lost his mobility. Losing his voice would have been a calamity he didn't think he could have lived with.

For years he had convinced himself that he was ready to die. He was no stranger to death. As a pastor he'd been at the bedside of many of his parishioners when they passed. Besides, he had lived a good life, had made a difference, and had believed he could pass off the scene with a certain amount of equanimity.

This brush with death revealed how wrong he had been. He didn't want his life to end. He couldn't be phlegmatic about his passing. He didn't want the world to carry on without him. Like a swimmer stepping out of a river and leaving no trace of his presence, the impermanence of his life unsettled him.

He wondered whether the Preacher's raging against the *hevel* of his life had occurred for reasons very similar to his. Over and over he spoke of no remembrance. And when he wasn't worried about that, the Preacher complained that all he had done would be undone by whoever took over after he was gone. In a short time a fool could ruin even great things.

The old man had always considered the Preacher a bit of a wimp concerning these things. Since his stroke, he had a greater appreciation for the Preacher's struggle to come to terms with this. Maybe he had been too hard on him.

# CHAPTER 23

The quiet words of the wise are more to be heeded than
the shouts of a ruler of fools.
—Ecclesiastes 9:17

The next few days were filled with intense effort and exhaustion. Every other day his physical therapist would spend an hour with him, forcing him beyond what he thought he could do. If it wasn't for the tangible progress, the old man would have given up. But he could tell he was slowly gaining strength and mobility.

Chris knocked on his door midmorning on Thursday.

"I need to make a confession," the young man said when he stepped into the room. "While you were in the hospital, I looked over some of your notes on Ecclesiastes. Let me know when you're ready to get back to work."

The old man knew his grandson was trying to encourage him by getting him engaged in writing again. The effort had worked well just a few weeks before.

He invited his grandson to take his usual place at the desk. The room remained much as it had been during all their previous sessions. The presence of the wheelchair, pulled up tight against the left side of his leather chair, stood as a silent testament to all that had changed since the three of them had met just over a week ago.

When he spoke, the old man did so clearly but slowly. What he said surprised his grandson.

"I think it's important to finish the book. You are going to have to do more of the legwork to make it happen. You can use my notes for my thinking up to this point."

He paused, processing his thoughts.

"What I want to focus on in the time I have left—" He stopped when the young man began to protest.

Starting again, he said, "What I want to focus on in the time I have left has more to do with living the book than just writing it. By that I mean the book of Ecclesiastes. There are some key verses I think might be saying something very important to me right now, and I need to figure them out."

"Can I help with that as well?" the young man asked.

"I don't think I could do it without you."

He looked at the young man across the small room. A trust had built up between them in the past several weeks. Something he was going to draw on now.

"However, in order for this to work, I need to move into your space a little bit."

"I'm not sure what you mean by that," his grandson replied. "What do you want to know?"

"The first day we spoke of working on the book, and then once again later, you shared a little of your journey. If you're comfortable sharing more, I think it would be helpful for our work to know where you are now."

It was the young man's turn to speak slowly, not with reluctance but with a thoughtful deliberateness of someone thinking as he was speaking.

"I guess there are two dimensions to where I am right now. The first is the problem of evil." He paused to frame his thoughts and then said, "Remember when I told you I was unsure why my father's leaving was such a powerful catalyst in the demise of my faith?"

The old man nodded.

"I think I've figured that out. The only way I can put it is to say my concerns are not just the problem of evil but also the problem of things that are just bad. It was our study of Ecclesiastes that put me on to this distinction. I discovered that the Hebrew word typically translated in the book as "evil" can also refer to something that is tragic or harmful. For me, I think of evil in strictly moral or ethical terms, related to but different from the bad things that happen in the world. My father's infidelity was immoral, but the consequences of my parent's divorce for the rest of us were just tragic.

"I know the distinction in this case is a little fuzzy, but a lot of bad happens in the world every day. Children die of cancer, accidents happen, twisters rip through neighborhoods. I don't think of these events as evil if they didn't come as a result of choice on someone's part.

"In my mind the problem of evil and the problem of bad are closely related when it comes to God—at least the God I used to believe in. In both cases He knew the evil and the bad that were going to happen to our family. He made a choice and could have done something about them but didn't. I couldn't live with the consequences of my own theology. If God *could* do something about things that were tragic or evil, then God *should* do something. It was as simple as that. I couldn't respect Him, and finally I didn't want to believe in a God like that."

The old man asked, "What is the second thing?"

Chris thought for a minute. "Do you remember when I was mad at myself for being angry with a God I didn't believe in?"

The old man smiled. "Yes, I do," he said.

"Well, I have had to be really honest with myself and conclude what was probably obvious to you. I was mad at God because I really still believed in Him. I didn't want to believe in a God who would allow the bad things to happen. But whether I like what He has or hasn't done—and I say this with both regret and embarrassment—I still believe in Him."

The old man couldn't have spoken if he had wanted to. Besides his appreciation for his grandson's honesty and his gratitude for the remnant of faith that remained, he felt a deep satisfaction that he may have made a difference.

After a moment of profound silence, the young man said, "I spoke of the God I used to believe in. That God has gone away. I'm not sure what the God I believe in now is really like. That is going to take some time to sort out."

"Chris," his grandfather said, "thank you for your honesty and trust. I'm not even going to comment on your last statement. I have confidence you will figure it out."

"I'm not so sure, but like you and the Preacher, I will work on it until I do."

The young man asked, "Why was it important for you to understand this?"

"I know you don't want to hear this, but I got a clear message from the doctor that my brain is like the state of California. We are both waiting for the big one to happen. It may be in a month. It may be in five years. Who knows, maybe it won't happen at all.

"But I have to plan as if it will happen. The next weeks and months are critical for me. I have to finish my work on Ecclesiastes as quickly as possible. Right now life is too precious, too compelling, to leave conversations unspoken. I can't do the work I need to with these questions unanswered.

"You are in a different place in your life than I am. Because of that, I need you to know where I'm coming from, and I need to know where you're coming from."

"I'm okay with that," the young man said. "So where does all of this leave us. It sounds as if we have a two-track process—me working on the book and both of us sorting out these verses."

"I don't think they are unrelated. The verses I'm wrestling with are key to understanding the book. As we sort them out, I think writing the book will be easier."

The old man sagged in his chair as he said, "I hate to admit this, but I'm beat. Let's come back to this tomorrow."

"Okay," said his grandson. "Would it be okay if Mom helped us some as well? I think she would really like to, and I think she could really help us as well."

Without hesitation, the old man said, "I would love that."

# CHAPTER 24

If the ax is dull and its edge unsharpened,
more strength is needed, but skill will
bring success. —Ecclesiastes 10:10

*W*hen he and his grandson had talked about getting together on Friday, he'd forgotten that he had a follow-up medical appointment late that afternoon after Emma got out of work. By the time she got home, he was already tired and in a bad mood.

Always well groomed, the old man struggled to shave himself using his left hand and an electric razor. He noticed that he'd missed some whiskers just above his collar line for a couple of days, and they were already noticeable. Along with bushy eyebrows and ear hair, overlooked whiskers were what he called "geezer issues" he had vowed to himself that he would never happen. And yet here they were, and he wasn't happy.

Dressing himself was also a challenge, though less so as time went on. Socks had become a problem because he was no longer using the appliance the occupational therapist had given him in the hospital. He was using two hands now, but his right one didn't have strength or fine motor skills yet. Buttoning his shirt and putting on his belt were difficult for the same reason. He waited for Emma to tie his shoes. It was still wing tips. He refused to get the black sport shoes with the Velcro tabs.

\* \* \* \* \*

"Dad, I'm home," Emma called when she came in the back door.

"I'm in here," he replied. She heard him mutter something about "geezer inspection."

"What's that?" she asked as she walked into his room.

"Oh, nothing. I'm just pulling my grumpy-old-man routine. Let me have a few minutes driving down a tree-lined street, and I'll be fine."

Standing in front of him, Emma did a brief inspection. She reached over and smoothed down an errant lock of hair. Kneeling down to tie his shoes, she noticed he had a spot of food on the front of his pants but didn't mention it.

They had talked the night before and decided that he would still use the wheelchair when going out in public, even though he was able to negotiate the house in his walker. The distance from the car to the office and back seemed a bit much for that.

Two hours later they were back home. They'd stopped at the deli on the way and picked up supper. While Emma set the table and dished out the food, her father rolled into his bedroom and transferred into his old leather chair.

When Emma called to him a few minutes later and got no response, she panicked a little. Quickly walking into his room, she found him asleep. Debating whether to wake him up, she decided against it. Going back into the kitchen, she covered the food and put it in the fridge. She would wait for him to awaken so they could eat together.

Walking to the stove, she began to heat some water for tea. When it was ready, she sat down in her chair and thought about the past week. Her father had made remarkable progress. Strength was returning to his right side, though the doctor warned that progress would slow as time went on. His speech was almost back to normal, and for that she was especially grateful. She couldn't imagine what it would have been like if he'd lost the ability to communicate.

He and Chris had reconnected and were already beginning to work on the book again. Something seemed to have changed in her son as well. She couldn't put her finger on it, but he seemed to be emerging from his fog a little bit and was more like his old self.

He didn't have to work tonight and had gone out with friends. But he wasn't pulling the all-nighters he'd had a few weeks ago. She would have to be patient and let him find his own way to tell her what was going on.

She got up and checked on her father. Taking the summer blanket off the foot of his bed, she gently covered him up as best she could. Looking at him as he slept, she thought again of how close she'd come to losing him. He did look better than he had a week ago. There was, however, an air of mortality that hung about him. The vulnerability he'd shown during the worst of the health crisis was fading, but there was a sense that he was living on borrowed time.

Gently tucking the blanket around his waist, she returned to the kitchen. Her tea had cooled to the point of tastelessness. Walking over to the sink, she poured it out, rinsed the cup, and put it in the dishwasher.

*How ironic*, she thought. Her life felt like that tea. First hot, then tepid, now cold. What was the point? Gil was gone. Kristen was a continent away. Chris would get his life back together. And her father had become the ridge pole, the house-band of her life. But how long would that last? Was there something wrong with her that she needed, perhaps wanted, a strong man in her life, even if it was her father? She was sure some of her friends would disapprove.

But it didn't seem like a gender thing as much as a relationship one. Life was good when she was in a relationship. Perhaps everyone was like that. As soon as she thought it, she realized the flaw in her thinking. Life may be good when she was in a relationship—if it was a good relationship. Her marriage hadn't been. Or, in the case of her parents, good relationships came to an end. Then what?

She remembered something her dad had told her when she got engaged. *You always have a choice. You need to be able to say, "I can live without him, but I choose to live with him." Sweetie, without that attitude, you may never become your own person.*

Like most engaged people, she was in love with love and had ignored his advice. Thirty years later she was going to have to give that level of independence another shot. It was a scary thought.

Looking at her watch, she decided to wake her father so he would be able to sleep tonight. Walking into his room, she could hear his deep breathing.

"Daddy?"

He stirred.

"Daddy, let's eat some supper before it gets too late."

# CHAPTER 25

As you do not know the path of the wind, or
how the body is formed in a mother's womb so
you cannot understand the work of God, the
Maker of all things. —Ecclesiastes 11:5

All three of them felt a little odd as they assembled in the old man's room on Sunday morning. It was as if an earthquake had rolled through since they'd met two weeks ago, and everything had fallen back into its original place. Well, almost everything.

The old man sat in his leather chair with his Bible on his lapboard, but his right arm was no longer the animated expression of his thoughts. Instead it lay quietly, though not immobile, on the board with the right thumb tucked into his fist rather than around it.

Chris sat behind the desk with his laptop open while his fingers played with the touch pad. His changes were less apparent but just as real. If one paid close attention, his words were the window to where the dust was settling in his life.

Emma was in her ladder-back chair with her Bible in her lap. Like chinks falling inside a cinder block wall during a temblor, her sense of vulnerability was largely out of sight.

The old man's opening comments sounded more formal than they were. "Thank you for coming," he said with deep sincerity. "It feels strange but right to have the three of us meeting together again. Not long ago, I thought the jig was up. Apparently that wasn't meant to be."

"Daddy, I can't tell you how happy I am that we're all here, relatively healthy, and working on your book."

He looked affectionately at both his daughter and grandson. "I'm feeling pretty good. I've made good progress, though I wish I was more mobile." Unconsciously, his eyes moved to the left, where the walker stood.

Slightly embarrassed, the old man said, "Enough of this sentimentalism. Let's get to work." Looking at his daughter, he said, "Emma, I told Chris earlier that I want him to continue to work on the book using the notes I've generated over the years. He has given me a draft of his work, and I like what I've read.

"What I would like us to do is talk about some key verses, puzzling ones actually, and see what we can make of them. Chris, like I told you, I'm more interested in living the words of the Preacher than just writing about them."

"Grandpa, I heard what you said, but I'm not sure what you meant."

"Okay, let me give an example from some verses from chapter four. One proverb in particular makes my point."

DON WILLIAMS

The old man carefully opened his Bible with his right hand and turned the pages with his left. He stopped and read, "Ecclesiastes chapter four, verses nine through twelve: 'Two are better than one, because they have a good return for their labor: If either of them falls down, one can help the other up. But pity anyone who falls and has no one to help them up. Also, if two lie down together, they will keep warm. But how can one keep warm alone? Though one may be overpowered, two can defend themselves. A cord of three strands is not quickly broken.'"

He looked up at Chris and said, "We could look at those verses historically or theologically, but what I need to do is live them. In fact, we are doing that right now. We are the three-stranded cord."

"Makes sense," Chris responded.

The old man continued, "There are three sets of verses I want us to talk about. One of them is right here in chapter seven, verse two." He turned a couple pages and read, "'It is better to go to a house of mourning than to go to a house of feasting, for death is the destiny of everyone; the living should take this to heart.'

"I know that seems like a bit of gallows humor, but even as a young man I was fascinated by what was being said here. It seemed so in your face. Is the Preacher being ironic or paradoxical, or is this hyperbole?"

He looked at his daughter. "From the perspective of someone who is fifty-something, what do you think he is saying?"

She opened her Bible and took a minute to read the first half of chapter seven. "I think the older I get, the less I need to hear this message, mainly because I think more about aging, and the previous generation is already passing off the scene. Sorry, Dad."

"Don't worry. I remember middle age very well, and you're right. My dad died when I was fifty-five. Chris, if I remember correctly, you minored in psychology in college. Isn't there something about the aging and death of a parent being the thing that throws men into a midlife crisis?"

The young man responded, "You're right about that theory being out there. However, I don't think everyone buys into the fact that it is a crisis for every man."

"Back to the text," Emma interjected. "I think the Preacher seems to be looking back from old age and wishing he'd thought a little more seriously about life when he was younger."

"If we're going to throw psychology around," Chris said, "I think that it's more Erik Erikson's Stages of Psychosocial Development. If we're going to shoehorn the Preacher into anything, I think he got to old age and experienced what Erikson identifies as despair rather than integrity. He evaluated his life, had regrets he couldn't come to terms with, and got depressed."

"I can see that," said the old man. "So Chris, your mom and I can make some sense of this from our time of life. What do you think from the perspective of your twenties?"

"Looking at the book as a whole, I'm convinced the author is targeting a younger audience. Think of the last chapter, which talks about remembering the Creator when you're young. So the Preacher uses a little hyperbole to get our attention. His statement that it's better to go to a wake than to a wedding was that slap in the face you talked about. The Preacher wants his audience to ask why."

"Dad," Emma said, "I remember when Mom was in hospice; I talked with one of the nurses about her work. I couldn't understand why someone would choose to do what she did. Her answer surprised me. She said, 'If you want to learn how to live, hang out with someone who is dying.' Maybe that is a modern way of saying what the Preacher is trying to tell us."

Her father answered, "I can attest to the fact that living in the valley of the shadow of death makes every moment of life more precious. There is a heightened appreciation for relationships. However, I question whether this is something that can be sustained, especially if you aren't the one facing your demise."

"I think there's a historical dimension to this we can't ignore." Chris had been taking notes. He stopped as he made the observation. "I'm guessing that life expectancy was a lot shorter then. Certainly infant mortality was higher."

"So how are you relating that to Ecclesiastes?" the old man asked.

"I'm thinking of your question for my generation. A lot of people my age have never even been to a funeral, and no one significant in their lives has died. So what do we do with the Preacher's challenge for them? If it had been written today, he might have said, 'Better to spend time with the poor than to party.'"

"This really presents an interesting challenge to any biblical concept," his grandpa responded. "How do we bring it into modern times and still do justice to the principle?"

"Maybe that is the place to start," Emma agreed. "What is the underlying principle here? Is it really about funerals and parties? Probably not."

Chris responded, "The Preacher does say in verse two that the living should take their mortality to heart. Perhaps the principle is to balance *carpe diem* with the broader view and deeper values of life."

His mother said, "Maybe these are two principles at work. One is that life is precious, and a sense of our mortality heightens that. The second grows out of that— treat life with respect."

"So it's like having twenty-twenty vision: the ability to see the long view and have it inform the present," her father explained. "Emma, I remember your grandfather telling me that on the farm the only way to plow a straight line was to keep your eye on the end of the field. Focusing on the ground in front of you was a formula for disaster."

"I want to come back to *carpe diem*," Chris said. "It seems to me that there are two kinds, and the Preacher addresses them both. The first approach is, seize the day because there is nothing else. When the Preacher made work or possessions the end in themselves, they were vanity. The second way is to seize the day with the end in view. It's like we said about the poem in chapter three. It isn't just our mortality we need to take into account but God as well." After a pause, he remarked, "I can't believe I'm the one saying this."

Each thought about this. Then the old man said, "Maybe we mined this verse enough for today. Sometime

I would like to talk about verses fifteen through eighteen. There the Preacher says not to be too holy or too bad. Is it possible to be too holy? And is it okay to be bad but not too bad? Until next time."

Chris closed his laptop and went back to his room as Emma carried her chair back to the kitchen, each pondering the old man's question.

# CHAPTER 26

However many years anyone may live, let
them enjoy them all. —Ecclesiastes 11:8

*W*ednesday evening found each of them engaged in separate but significant activities. After supper the old man spent a half hour doing his strengthening and range-of-motion exercises. He was always tired at the end of the day but did his workout then believing that was when it would do him the most good. Like a marathon runner hitting the wall at twenty miles, he knew the one who pushed through the tiredness and pain made it to the finish line.

Completing his exercises, he began to get ready for bed. Changing into his pajamas remained an ordeal, mostly because he made no concessions to right-side weakness. Moving into his bathroom, he grasped the toothbrush in his right hand, loaded on the toothpaste, and began trying the circular motions he had used so easily to clean his teeth for seventy years. He knew he would likely hear from his dentist about plaque buildup.

To wash his face, he carefully positioned the washcloth on his right hand and turned on the hot water with his left. Wringing out the washcloth reminded him that it wasn't just motor skills that needed improvement but strength as well.

When he was finished he carefully walked to his bedroom door, keeping the wall within reach. Sitting at the table, grading homework, Emma looked up when he said good night. She got up, went over, gave him a hug, and kissed his forehead.

"Love you, Dad," she said.

"Love you too, sweetie," he replied.

Slowly making his way to the bed, he pulled back the covers and lay down. Getting under them and pulling them back up took some effort, but he did it. With his left hand, he reached over and turned out the light. Glancing at the clock, he saw that it was 8:30, his usual bedtime.

Lying in the dark, he was shocked to realize he hadn't thought of Sarah one time that day. Though his head told him it was inevitable, his heart quaked with guilt at what he'd done. He chastised himself for something that felt as unpardonable as it was predictable. If he was doing this five months out, what would it be like by the end of a year?

His remorse cued the words "no remembrance" in his mind. He was struck by the thought that this wasn't just a commentary on his being forgotten. He was the one guilty of doing the forgetting. More than anyone else, he should be the docent for Sarah's life. He had been so consumed with his own issues and interests that he'd neglected this most precious task. Maybe he should abandon the writing project. He suspected he was becoming too obsessed with it. Before drifting off to sleep, he decided he would talk with Emma about it in the morning.

* * * * *

After saying good night to her father, Emma turned off the overhead light in the kitchen and sat with a cup of mandarin spice tea in the warm light of the table lamp. The day had brought the closing of an era in her life. She and her father had transferred the funds to pay Gil for his half of the house. Late in the afternoon, with power of attorney from her father, she and her lawyer had met with Gil and his lawyer.

She wasn't surprised with how angry she felt when she saw Gil again. It was, she knew, an expression of the hurt and shame festering deep in her heart. Like her father, she had healed enough to go for periods of time without thinking of the former object of her affection. Rather than guilt, she felt relief with her incremental step of progress.

Sitting across the table from him, she'd been repulsed by everything about him. He was nothing but a poser. His lame comb-over fooled no one. His expensive suit looked like it didn't have enough material to cover his growing waistline. The cuffs of his shirt were monogramed, but the collar was so tight, she was sure he was killing brain cells. At least she hoped he was. Even the sound of his voice nauseated her, and she had to force herself to look him in the eye.

She thought smugly to herself, *Vanity, thy name is Gil.* That was a good one. She would have to tell her father about her new interpretation of *hevel*. In spite of all this, she got through the ordeal, and the house was theirs, free and clear.

Sitting in the kitchen and analyzing the day she was struck by the irony of forgetting. She wanted to preserve the memory of her mother and delete the memory of her ex. Sadly, love seemed to be less potent than anger in fixing things in her mind.

In this case her anger wasn't just directed at Gil. As she gained more insight, she became more upset with herself. Right now, however, her self-awareness seemed to be only that. She could not identify one change she had made in her life as a result of owning what she'd done. It seemed like the only changes that had taken place had been done *to* her, not *by* her—the empty place in her bed, the single-income status, the changes she'd seen in her social life because of no longer being a couple.

Rather than beating herself up, which was her natural response, she wondered what changes she expected to see. More independence? More honesty? As she thought about it, perhaps the growth needed to come in more internal ways. More self-acceptance. More satisfaction not only with her life but also with herself. And probably less fear about facing life alone. When put in those terms, she decided maybe she had made progress.

She thought again of the text her father had read in Ecclesiastes 4. It had painted a pretty bleak picture of being alone. In her case she was alone as a divorcée but not alone in terms of family and friends and people she cared about—and who cared about her. Her bed was empty, like the Preacher said, and that wasn't going to change, at least not in the foreseeable future. She had to assume the empty bed was a metaphor for an empty life, and what she did about that was up to her.

Emma wondered what advantage she might find in the single life beyond the obvious relief of being away from an abusive, cheating husband. What would the Preacher say about the fact that it was her partner who had pushed her down and that there had been a coldness in her marital bed even when he was there? She guessed that, like any proverb, those verses were stating a general, obvious truth that must be applied in situations that were much more complicated in real life.

She got up, rinsed out her cup, and put it in the sink. It occurred to her that the Preacher had left something out—whether she was part of a two- or three-strand cord; it would never be one. She knew that however mysterious His presence was, God was there. What was it the psalmist had said? "A present help in time of need." With that comforting thought, she got ready for bed.

* * * * *

Chris got home at about one o'clock after having a few drinks after work with his friends. He'd texted his mom about what time he would likely get home. He would have been pleased to know that once she'd heard from him, she'd gone to bed and was asleep by the time he pulled in the driveway.

As he got ready for bed, he admitted to himself that while he still enjoyed going out with his friends, the drinking had become tiresome, especially the amount consumed. Early on he'd welcomed the social lubrication. He had even found himself going to the bar alone some evenings. Sitting there with a few beers under his belt gave him a feeling of well-being and belonging. The convivial atmosphere seemed to be just what he needed as he transitioned into the unknown. He thought he could see himself making the bar his social anchor point just as church had been.

Reconnecting with his grandfather, however, had changed all that. Their open, meaningful conversations had made the ones at the bar seem superficial and irrelevant. His grandfather's stroke and the evenings spent at the hospital had broken the cycle of being with his friends from work. He realized it wasn't a funeral and a party but a hospital and a bar that had helped him understand what was really important in his life. And while he didn't see himself going back to church, he understood that he was reopening the door to a relationship with God he'd thought was closed forever.

# CHAPTER 27

Let them remember the days of darkness,
for there will be many. Everything to come
is meaningless. —Ecclesiastes 11:8 b.c

The next morning at breakfast, the old man told his daughter his regret for not thinking about her mother for a whole day.

"I catch myself having to consciously remember what her voice sounded like," Emma said. "That is really sad."

He thought about her words a minute and decided he couldn't let her experience excuse his guilt. "But she was the love of my life, and she's only been gone five months. It's unforgivable."

"Daddy, you have to move on."

"I'm sorry, but that sounds like psychobabble. Closure, getting stuck, moving on, what does all that mean anyway? They're just labels someone made up to sell books or platitudes you might hear on Dr. Phil just before a commercial break."

"But what can you do about it," Emma questioned. "If we believed in ancestor worship, we would set up an altar to the loved one who has passed. There is something both sweet and spooky about that. I'm not sure you want to go there."

"I was thinking it was my obsession with writing the book that had brought this about. What would you think if I gave it a rest?"

He could tell his words shocked her.

"You said yourself that this project isn't about a book. It's about life. Writing the book has helped heal your heart. It's built a bridge you and your grandson can walk on. It has provided a context for the three of us to talk about some very meaningful things.

"One thing I haven't heard you ask is, what would Mom want you to do? If you were the one who died first, what would you want her to do?"

Her words bothered him, not because they were inappropriate but because of their truth. He felt a visceral wrenching. It felt like letting go, part two.

One night, months ago, as he'd sat by Sarah's bed, he realized he needed to give her permission to go. He hadn't even been sure she could hear or understand, but he told her how much he loved her and would always love her. He told her how wonderful their life together had been. And then he told her it was all right for her to go, that she would always be in his heart and that they would see each other again in a better place.

She died that night.

The old man looked up at his daughter. "You have the gift of carrying your mother's DNA. I just realized that in a different way I do too. Everything I am and everything I have accomplished with my life, I owe to her."

Tears of love and sadness washed over his cheeks. "I may not have her genes, but she is as much a part of me as if I did."

They sat for a few quiet moments at the old oak table, thinking about the richness of their lives because of this woman, this mother, this wife.

The old man broke the reverie. "Maybe remembrance isn't just about memory. Maybe as we live our lives, as we move on, we become more of what she helped us to be. We honor her in unspoken, maybe even unconscious, ways. Is that rationalizing?"

"I don't think so."

And so for the second time, the old man let go. The first time had been letting go of Sarah's physical presence. The second time was more intangible. He wasn't sure whether he could put into words what it meant. It felt like casting off from a dock and drifting into uncharted waters. And it was just as hard as the first time.

"I don't know if you ever knew that your grandmother went to your grandfather's graveside every week. She took a chair and would sit there and talk with him. We all thought she was losing it. I think I get it now. She had to let him go in death, but she couldn't let the second time to move on with her life."

Emma got up and walked over to her father's side. Laying her hand on his shoulder, she said, "I have to get out the door. Are you going to be okay?"

"Better than you might think. Thanks for listening to an old man's ruminations."

"Can't think of any better way to start the day," Emma said with a smile. She cleared the table and finished getting ready for the day.

Seated in the leather chair back in his room, the old man thought about the words "moving on." What did they mean anyway? They sounded like leaving someone behind, and that didn't seem quite right. He supposed in a situation like Emma's divorce, leaving someone behind was the point. For him, moving on didn't have to mean leaving Sarah behind. She was so much a part of him that he wasn't sure that was even possible. He needed to move on with his life, conscious not only of her presence but also of her contribution. She would always be with him.

# CHAPTER 28

Follow the ways of your heart and whatever your
eyes see, but know that for all these things God
will bring you into judgment. —Ecclesiastes 11:9

The meeting in the old man's room the next
weekend was beginning to feel like a ritual
but a good one that helped pace the week and give the
participants something to look forward to.

On Friday, the assignment was given to read chapter
nine and be prepared to talk especially about verse eleven.

The old man began by referring them to an earlier
verse. "Before we get started, I want to make a comment
about verse nine. The irony of it always tickles me." He
opened his Bible and read, "'Enjoy life with your wife,
whom you love, all the days of this meaningless life that
God has given you under the sun—all your meaningless
days. For this is your lot in life and in your toilsome labor
under the sun.'"

He chuckled. "It's like he is saying, 'Have a meaningful
time with your lovely wife in your meaningless life.' Talk

about dialectic. He puts both the good and the bad in one verse."

Turning to his grandson, he said, "Chris, would you read verse eleven?"

The young man opened his Bible and read, "'I have seen something else under the sun: The race is not to the swift or the battle to the strong, nor does food come to the wise or wealth to the brilliant or favor to the learned; but time and chance happen to them all.'"

"I think," the old man said, "this is not only the most radical verse in the book, but it may also be the fulcrum on which it all rests. So maybe a good place to start is for each of us to say how this verse might or might not fit into our view of God."

Chris began, "First of all, this really flies in the face of where I used to be. I saw God controlling everything. And to me that's different from being in control of everything. That may seem like splitting hairs, but the difference seems significant to me. However, I don't know how to reconcile my current view with one of the big principles in the Old Testament—'Obey and live; disobey and die.'"

"What I don't get," his mother said, "is how the idea of chance fits into a universe with a loving God. Is He really going to let something random be the determining factor in peoples' fates? It doesn't make sense."

"Take my stroke, please." The old man smiled at his version of the vaudeville joke. Holding up his right hand, he said, "Was my stroke part of God's plan? Was it a result of some disobedience or need for discipline from God? Or, as the Preacher seems to be saying, is it just one of those things that happened because of my clogged arteries?"

"A couple years ago," Chris said, "I read a book on chaos theory, which, by the way, is poorly named. It isn't that there aren't laws or things that can't be understood from cause to effect, as the title implies. What that theory says is that in many situations, there are too many variables for us to understand or predict all of what is going on.

"I think it started with this guy trying to create a computer model that would predict the weather. What he found was that there were way too many variables to predict the weather more than five to seven days out."

His mother said, "So what does chaos theory have to do with Ecclesiastes?"

"I think Chris is on to something," the old man said. "Maybe the word *chance* is like the word *chaos*. Both can be easily misinterpreted. Perhaps the Preacher was saying that there are things that don't follow a straight-line cause and effect, like the fastest person winning the race. Maybe the runner had the flu the night before or got a stone in his shoe. There are things beyond the knowing of the observers as well as the runners themselves that may seem like a chance occurrence.

"Anyway, one of the themes of Ecclesiastes is that human knowledge is very limited. Remember in chapter three how the Preacher said we may want to understand the big picture, but it would be far from us."

"I have always been comforted," Emma said, "by the fact that God is in control, that He has a plan."

"But Emma, think about what Chris said earlier. God may have a plan, but He allows us the free will to make choices within that plan. Just because He has a plan doesn't mean He controls everything."

"But doesn't the Bible say there is a judgment, a second coming, and heaven? Aren't those God's plans, and wouldn't He have to be in control to make them happen?"

"Yes," her son responded. "He would have to be in control but not controlling everything to make the happen. Let's go back to Grandpa's stroke. God can have a plan for Grandpa's life, like to be in heaven. But He could allow something like a stroke to happen without causing it, because it wouldn't take Grandpa outside His will for him."

"As the stroke victim, let me weigh in on this. Several things seem to be true for me in this situation. One, God wants me to have a relationship with Him, both now and in eternity. Two, He has allowed bad things to happen without being the direct cause of those things. Three, while I believe God can and does intervene in the world with what we call miracles, usually He simply allows life to proceed unchecked."

His daughter wasn't satisfied with his answer. "But I come back to my earlier point. Where is God in those everyday events, whether in the birth of a baby or in a stroke?"

"Aren't we back in the poem in chapter three with this?" her father said. "Birth and death and strokes all happen because of the laws God established to run the universe. His role beyond establishing those laws is to be with us when these things happen. He's not absent just because He's silent."

Chris had been quiet through the last exchange. These issues lay at the heart of his struggle with a good

God standing by while bad things happened, not just to good people but to innocent ones as well.

"Let me talk this out," Chris said. "First of all, time and chance may be the Preacher's way of saying we won't always be able to understand cause and effect. But He isn't saying things are just random. Second, God can have a role other than that of prime mover. It isn't a question of Him either causing or not caring. He can allow free will to happen and to be there to help us pick up the pieces. Am I making sense?"

"Makes sense to me," his grandfather said.

Emma wasn't convinced. "So what does that do with the biblical principle you mentioned earlier about 'Obey and live, disobey and die'?"

Her father responded, "I'm not sure I have a complete answer to that, but here's what I think. 'Obey and live' means I'm living within the laws of life God has established. And in that sense I'm living within His will for me. Obedience doesn't mean no bad things will happen. Nor does it mean that if I disobey, I will die that day.

"When I obey, I put myself in a place where I can receive God's blessing, comfort, and guidance. Disobedience not only puts me at cross-purposes with the laws of life but also puts me in a place where I'm unable to receive God's blessings. A friend of mine once said, 'Obedience increases the odds that good things will happen, but it doesn't guarantee they will.' Maybe that is the chance the Preacher is talking about."

"So," Chris said, "it looks like I've been guilty of putting God in a box where He doesn't belong. The fact that bad things happen doesn't mean He is absent. He is just present in different ways.

"Maybe it's like Adam and Eve in the garden. They were told the laws that were operating. They chose to ignore them. If I remember from one of my Old Testament classes, the verse doesn't say, 'In the day you eat thereof you will die.' It says, 'In dying you will die.' The dying process will begin.

"God was active as the lawmaker. He established the consequences of free will, and then when Adam and Eve chose to break the law and the relationship, He went out in search of them. He played the role not of enforcer but of seeker."

They all sat, quietly thinking about this. Finally the old man spoke. "Are we being fair to the text and to God? We can spin whatever sounds nice, but does it line up with Scripture, and can it be lived in practical terms?"

"This is all very personal for me," Chris said. "I'm not sure I can play the theologian here."

Emma responded, "It is certainly different than the role I saw God playing. It would allow for free will and an active, caring God. I'd like to talk more about this next time."

Her father said, "That's fine. I do want to finish our discussions with a look at chapter twelve and the final poem about remembering our Creator when we are young."

Nodding their agreement, they packed up their things, and each moved on to his or her agendas for the rest of the day.

A dull headache tempered the old man's deep sense of satisfaction. After lunch he told Emma he was going to lie down for a short nap.

Later that afternoon, when she came in from working in the yard, she was surprised he wasn't up yet. After drinking a glass of cold water, she went to his door and knocked.

"Hey, sleepyhead. It's time to get up."

She listened and heard nothing. Opening the door, she called out quietly, "Daddy?"

No response. She walked over to the bed where her father appeared to be sleeping peacefully. She shook him and realized something was wrong.

"Daddy."

She touched the hand lying outside the covers. It was cold. Her knees buckled as she cried out, "Daddy!"

# CHAPTER 29

Now all has been heard; here is the conclusion of the
matter: Fear God and keep his commandments, for
this is the duty of all mankind. —Ecclesiastes 12:13

*A*s the morning sun filtered through the curtains,
it failed to brighten the room, which now felt
bereft of warmth and life. Sitting in his grandfather's
chair, Chris thought it should be called the "mourning
sun"—something able to illuminate without lightening.

It had taken an act of the will to come back into the
bedroom only two days after his grandfather's death. He
wasn't sure of all that drove him there. Perhaps it was the
simple desire to be close to the last place where the old
soul had animated the world. Now that he was here, the
weight of that loss pinned him to the chair, making it
difficult to move or even breathe.

How could everything look the same when nothing
was? In front of him was the desk where he had sat for
so many hours—talking, typing, trying to sort out the
meaning of life. His life. On its top lay the file folder with

the book manuscript that seemed to have aged since their last session. It was as if he could see the dust of time and disintegration accumulating before his eyes. How could something so fresh be ancient history already?

In the hours since the world had changed, his mind kept coming back to the last assignment his grandfather had given him. Looking down, he saw the lapboard and beside it, the Bible. Picking up the board and placing the Bible on top of it, he opened the book and turned to Ecclesiastes 12.

> Remember your Creator in the days of your youth, before the days of trouble come and the years approach when you will say, "I find no pleasure in them"—before the sun and the light and the moon and the stars grow dark, and the clouds return after the rain; when the keepers of the house tremble, and the strong men stoop, when the grinders cease because they are few, and those looking through the windows grow dim; when the doors to the street are closed and the sound of grinding fades; when people rise up at the sound of birds, but all their songs grow faint; when people are afraid of heights and of dangers in the streets; when the almond tree blossoms and the grasshopper drags itself along and desire no longer is stirred. Then people go to their eternal home and mourners go about the streets.
>
> Remember him—before the silver cord is severed, and the golden bowl is broken;

> before the pitcher is shattered at the spring,
> and the wheel broken at the well, and the
> dust returns to the ground it came from,
> and the spirit returns to God who gave it,
> "Meaningless! Meaningless!" says the [Pr]
> eacher. "Everything is meaningless!"

*How ironic*, Chris thought. *Remember.* They had often talked of being remembered, fearful of the time when no one would know they had even existed. Looking at the text before him, he was struck by this different type of remembering. Not a self-focused, navel-gazing remembrance. It was a remembrance of something by Someone who never forgot. Someone whose presence brought beauty and eternity to life. Someone whose Presence was there when remembering made all the difference.

The young man knew that in a few years he would be the stooped old man trembling at the well. But here was One who would never forget, never move on to something more important. Slowly the weight began to lighten. And with it came the faintest glimmer of hope that as ephemeral as it all might be, all wasn't *hevel.*

Carefully replacing the Bible and lapboard, he stood up. Walking over to the desk, he picked up the folder, tucked it under his arm, and left the room, closing the door behind him.

\* \* \* \* \*

Emma had avoided going into her father's room. The closed door off the kitchen helped her compartmentalize her pain—wall it off out of sight, if not out of mind. But it was Friday afternoon, and the man from the funeral home would be here in an hour to pick up the clothes her father would be buried in.

Putting down her cup of tea and pushing back her chair, she levered herself to her feet and walked reluctantly to the door. The knob felt cold in her hand as she turned it and walked in. She had been afraid the room would smell like death, whatever that was. Instead it had the rich, aged smell of old books. Of words and wisdom.

Leaving off the overhead light, she walked quietly over to the closet. Pulling open the folded door, she turned on the closet light. The smell of her father's cologne overwhelmed her. Tears began to flow. She no longer cared that her face was blotchy, that her nose ran and her tears left little marks on the front of her blouse. What amazed her was their unending supply. It was as if her head had been transformed into a reservoir for grief. She felt that if she could just cry it out, she could drain herself of all thought and feeling. Maybe then she could go on.

Sorting through the clothes, she picked out his tweed sport coat, a white shirt, and dark-blue pants. Bending down, Emma picked up his black wing tips. Something told her that shoes and socks were unnecessary, but she couldn't stand the thought of him going barefoot to the grave. It seemed undignified, uncaring.

She wondered whether she should get underwear for him. The thought of it made her smile. It was the type of thing her father would have gotten a chuckle out of. She decided she would send him to his eternal rest fully clothed.

Laying the items on the foot of the bed, she sat in her father's leather chair. She realized this was the first time she'd ever done so. The thought of it was somehow comforting, not just to be where he had experienced so much pleasure, but today it felt like taking her rightful place. It didn't look like a throne, but somehow she knew she was sitting on the ancestral seat, that she was now at the front of a long line that stretched behind her into the dim past.

Looking around the room, she saw the picture of her mother and father in front of the cathedral. They looked so happy standing there, holding hands. *A two-stranded cord*, she thought. Well, they would be united again.

To her surprise, Emma was neither envious nor empty at the thought. She knew her life was, in some mysterious way, still entwined with theirs. Just as hers was with her children and grandchildren. She wasn't alone. Picking up the clothes, she walked out of the room and closed the door.

# EPILOGUE

*T*he memorial service took place the next Sunday at Emma's church. The old man hadn't wanted an open casket, so his mortal remains dressed in his tweed sport coat, open-collared white shirt, dark blue pants, and wing tips rested quietly behind the coffin lid. The crowd was small. He had outlived many of his friends and all the family of his generation. A few of his former church members had driven the seventy-five miles to attend the funeral. His ex-son-in-law sat alone in the back row.

In their little island of sorrow on the front row, Emma and her two children were unaware of anything going on behind them. Kristen had flown in the night before, leaving her two children with her husband. After she'd unpacked, the three of them had sat around the kitchen table, talking. Out of habit, they were at their usual places. The fourth spot was empty.

They first went over the memorial service. The rest of the evening was spent in tears and laughter as they remembered good times with Grandma and Grandpa. Before they went to bed after midnight, they agreed no one would wear black the next day.

Now Emma sat on the pew between her two children, clutching a wadded-up tissue. Kristen held her mother's right hand in both of hers. Chris kept jiggling his knee and checking his inside coat pocket.

Following a prayer by Emma's pastor, Kristen walked slowly up to the pulpit, opened her Bible, and said in a sweet clear voice, "My grandfather loved Ecclesiastes. I want to read from chapter three in the New International Version.

> There is a time for everything, and a season
> for every activity under the heavens:
> a time to be born and a time to die,
> a time to plant and a time to uproot,
> a time to kill and a time to heal,
> a time to tear down and a time to build,
> a time to weep and a time to laugh,
> a time to mourn and a time to dance,
> a time to scatter stones and a time to gather
> them,
> a time to embrace and a time to refrain from
> embracing,
> a time to search and a time to give up,
> a time to keep and a time to throw away,
> a time to tear and a time to mend,
> a time to be silent and a time to speak,
> a time to love and a time to hate,
> a time for war and a time for peace.
>
> What do workers gain from their toil?
> I have seen the burden God has laid on the
> human race.

He has made everything beautiful in its time.
He has also set eternity in the human heart;
yet no one can fathom what God has done
from beginning to end.

I know that there is nothing better for people
than to be happy and to do good while they
live. That each of them may eat and drink,
and find satisfaction in all their toil—this is
the gift of God."

When she finished, Kristen closed her Bible and walked down the steps. Her mother met her at the bottom, and they embraced. Kristen continued to her seat as Emma climbed the steps to the pulpit. Before she spoke, she looked quietly out at those who had come. She hid her surprise at seeing her ex-husband in the back row.

Struggling to get her emotions in check, she began with a quaver in her voice. "Thank you for coming. Daddy would have been surprised and pleased.

"My fondest memories of my father come from my elementary and middle school years. He was the best father any girl could want. Always the safe harbor in the storms of pre-adolescence, I knew I had his full attention whenever I needed a listening ear.

"One night when I was ten, I remember him coming into my room after mom had tucked me in. I rested my head in the crook of his arm as he lay on top of the blanket. We talked about the day at school. Then my mind turned philosophical, and I asked him about God and eternity. I wanted to know what was beyond the edge of the universe and what happened before the beginning of time.

"He answered each of my inquiries as best he could and then told me there were some things only God knows. We spent probably a half hour talking with our pauses growing longer until both of us fell asleep. Mom had to come in and wake him up to go to bed."

Looking at her ex in the back, she said, "Losing someone you love, for whatever reason, is a terrible thing. When my mother passed away six months ago, I wondered if my father would be able to carry on. He did, and in doing so, he taught me that what has been torn can be mended. Like the patchwork quilt on his bed at home, in God's time something beautiful can be made of our lives again."

With a final look at the audience, Emma went down the stairs, paused, and touched the casket. She returned to her seat, feeling that perhaps she had begun the second letting go.

Chris stood, leaned over, gave his mother a tight hug, and mounted the steps. Adjusting the microphone, he looked over the crowd for the first time and saw some of his mom's friends and coworkers. He was surprised to see two of his new friends from the bookstore. In the dim light of the sanctuary, he saw his father sitting at the back. He couldn't look at his mother or the coffin.

Spreading out his notes, he said, "Some of you knew my grandfather, Joe Meeker. Many of you didn't. I would like to give you a sense of who he was and what he meant to those of us who loved him.

"He spent his life as a preacher and for forty years was involved in the lives of his congregation. As important as that was to him, it was his family who meant the most.

None of us ever felt that parishioners took precedence over family. Nor was he one who wore one mantle at work and another at home. He always brought himself to every situation.

"In reality there was nothing about Joe Meeker that would have made anyone notice him in a crowd. Average height, normal looks, quiet voice. He was content to make a difference in his small corner of a big world."

He stopped as his voice faltered. He continued, "Some may not have seen him as a man's man. But to me he was something more than that. His strength of character was shown through humility and love rather than domination and control. He taught me what it is to be human.

"My mom and I had the privilege of being with him during the final months of his life. It was a difficult time for each of us. I was in the midst of a crisis of faith. That didn't matter a whit to him. He found a way to engage me in conversations that have been the most important in my life.

"At the suggestion of my mother, he began to write a book on Ecclesiastes. Sadly he did not live to finish it. I think he knew that might happen, so during the last few times the three of us met, he said he would rather live the message of Ecclesiastes than write about it." He stopped and cleared his throat.

"So as I finish I would like to honor his memory by sharing how he lived the book.

Joe Meeker knew that work and family were gifts of God. He believed that to stay within God's will meant to live according to God's timing and guidance. He was humble about how much any of us can understand God and His plans. He never lost sight of what was really important in life. If he needed to go to a funeral rather than a party, he was there. He knew that God is known more through His presence than His miracles."

As Chris looked down at the casket for the first time, he worked to gain control of his emotions.

"And so, Grandpa, we say good-bye. We commit ourselves not just to remember you but to honor you by living our lives as you did—with honesty, integrity, and love."

# DISCUSSION QUESTIONS

1. What was it about Ecclesiastes that attracted the old man to study it so much?
2. How did the age of the family members affect their views or interpretations of Ecclesiastes?
3. What is the theme of Ecclesiastes?
4. What does *hevel* mean in Ecclesiastes?
5. In your opinion, what would make life *hevel*?
6. What is life "under the sun" like, according to the Preacher? Do you agree with him?
7. What was the point of the Preacher's experiment in Ecclesiastes 2? Did it accomplish what he wanted it to?
8. According to the Preacher, how are various events in life made beautiful?
9. Was Emma right in believing the Preacher might be a woman hater?
10. What was Chris's crisis of faith really all about?
11. According to the Preacher, why is it better to go to a funeral than to a party?
12. How do the Preacher's views on "time and chance" fit with the life of faith?

13. What do you think about the old man's concept of the "second leaving" as it relates to grieving?

14. Would you agree with the Preacher's characterization of God's presence in the world?

15. Is Ecclesiastes a pessimistic, optimistic, or realistic book? Why?

16. How would you characterize Chris's faith by the end of the book?

17. What progress did Emma make with her issues of being alone?

18. What dimensions of remembering are discussed in Ecclesiastes?

19. What did the old man mean by "living the book" of Ecclesiastes?

20. How can the approach to life in Ecclesiastes be reconciled with what is found in the rest of the Bible?

21. Do you believe the Preacher believed in heaven? Why?

22. What do you think of the idea that because God is silent in a given situation it does not mean He is not present?

23. Is it legitimate to have a wide variety of interpretations of Ecclesiastes based on a reader's age, gender, or personal experiences? Why?

24. Why would a book like Ecclesiastes be included in the Bible?